# Auld Claes an' Porridge

## Mhairi Livingstone Ross

*Best wishes
Mhairi Livingstone Ross
Molly Livingstone*

Bright Pen

Visit us online at www.authorsonline.co.uk

A Bright Pen Book

Text Copyright © Mhairi Livingstone Ross 2009

Cover design by Mhairi Livingstone Ross ©

All rights reserved. No part of this publication may be reproduced, stored in a retrieval system, or transmitted in any form or by any means, electronic, mechanical, photocopy, recording or otherwise, without prior written permission of the copyright owner. Nor can it be circulated in any form of bindming or cover other than that in which it is published and without similar condition including this condition being imposed on a subsequent purchaser.

ISBN 978-07552-1139-5

Authors OnLine Ltd
19 The Cinques
Gamlingay, Sandy
Bedfordshire SG19 3NU
England

This book is also available in e-book format, details of which are available at www.authorsonline.co.uk

## For Molly

*my beloved, irrepressible, matchless Mum
and the good folk of Moray who moulded her.*

## For Johnny

*my adored, gentle, loving Dad whom I miss so much.*

# Biography

## Mhairi Livingstone Ross

Mhairi Livingstone Ross was born in Oban and educated at Rockfield, Oban High School, Edinburgh University and Jordanhill College of Education.

She has worked in education, both special needs and mainstream, teaching in a large primary school in Oban as a Senior Teacher for many years.

After the restructuring of the education system, she was offered early retirement, enabling more time to be freed up for her many interests.

Married with two sons and two grandsons, she divides her time between family commitments, singing with Oban Gaelic Choir, historical research and writing for local interest groups.

She has contributed to a variety of local history projects, including interpretative boards for the area, articles for the local library and museum and has had a number of articles published by a Scottish interest magazine. Auld Claes an' Porridge is her first book.

Over the years, she and her husband have climbed all the Munros, trekked in the Alps, Pyrenees, Norway and New Zealand but more than anything, enjoy getting about and discovering their own beautiful country.

She enjoys cycling, skiing, ceilidh dancing and music. She also dabbles in gardening, enjoys the challenge of cryptic crosswords and reads extensively.

# Foreword

Anyone who feels hard done to by a glitch in the economy should read this book and those sitting pretty should read it too.

It is the history of a family in the first half of last century, generation by generation. It seems incredible to us nowadays to read of the poverty that was taken for granted. There were no social workers. There was no free medical care. A sick child might find a hospital bed, but that was all. You will notice the word 'might'. In this history sick children died and only sometimes survived. These were our people, flesh of our flesh, blood of our blood. I grieve and hammer the keys with fury as I think of the conditions they suffered. Today the diseases of childhood are only names, the names of the baby-saving vaccines. Seventy years ago the diseases themselves were present in every household.

Because this is a story of an agricultural community these houses were also haunted by hunger, not that it was any better in the towns. Yet in the country there was a community of body and spirit. There was always something for someone else. How neighbour assisted neighbour will warm the heart of every reader. Moray, on that long cold shoulder of Scotland is the seat of most of this and in particular the Strath of Dallas inland from Lossiemouth. We read how several generations won a slender living from the soil.

Much of the story is about the children. I read it with a feeling of loss. This is the downside of the British Empire on which the sun never set. Yet here if a child was hungry they were never fed on the fat of the land. A trip to the seaside was a treat. Education was there for every child but only of a sort. We learn how even the ablest children could not raise their eyes in ambition beyond the end of primary school. Secondary education was denied them and it was as if universities didn't exist. What a waste! What a waste!

What then did they do, these children of the land to whom so much was denied? If they were boys they fended for themselves as small tenant farmers. The alternative was employment as farm labourers, employed for half a year for a few pounds at a feeing fair. For the girls there was only 'service', another word for slaving for the rich in their large houses, the product of the wealth of Empire.

The wealth of Empire was not for the likes of them. We get only a glimpse and a hint of it. So and so was a good landowner. He was kind to his tenants. Mhairi Livingstone Ross has no bitterness in her. But what was in it for them, these children of the poor? Alas the Empire provided for such people ever more poverty.

Fast forward to Oban and we get a glimpse of an old soldier. His pension was a brass badge which authorised him to act as a porter on railway and pier in the hope of getting tips from people little better off than himself. That was the reward of Imperial service. On his death, leaving a young family, his widow had to hand in the brass badge and got in return thirty pieces of copper, half a crown as it was then called. Thirty pieces of copper for a soldier's widow. Thirty pieces of silver was another price for another betrayal. The author of this Foreword remembers elderly men with these badges. I hammer the keys with anger at proud soldiers reduced to a beggarly job as their reward for serving the Raj for half a lifetime. As for the dead soldier's family his grandson went barefoot from March to October and was provided with winter boots by a charity. This was within the lifetime of many still living, of mine for a start.

Yet this Foreword is the only angry part of this book. In life we are wise if we can take what is given to us and be thankful for it. That is how things were. That is how Mhairi Livingstone Ross saw them. That is how she puts them down in her clear limpid prose. She has given us a straightforward narrative with no special pleading. Her father, no longer a young man, was taken at St. Valery with the 51$^{st}$ Highland Division and suffered five years in a prison camp. He had a vivid memory and she has a vivid pen. The retreat to St. Valery is told with the clarity of memory of one who never forgot it. On his return he found his place in Oban Pipe Band. In Oban Station Hotel a Moray lass worked as a chambermaid.

One cannot but be glad to know that after such sufferings two people from such harsh backgrounds met, married and had a happy life.

Mhairi Livingstone Ross is their daughter. Her book is here to prove that happiness can be won from the harshest circumstances.

*Ian Hamilton Q.C.*

# Acknowledgements

Many people have helped in a variety of ways with the research for this book. I would like to thank them all.
Molly Skene (now Livingstone), my mother, for being herself.Bella Skene (now McCabe), for being herself and still a wonderful lady and the best auntie. The late Meg Tough, Elgin, daughter of Lizzie Masson, my grandmother's younger sister, an inspirational lady. Ian Tough, Garmouth, for help with the Masson side of the family. The staff at Elgin Library and, in particular, Linda Geddes, Margaret Heron and Graeme Wilson of the Local Heritage Centre for their patience and help. Eleanor Rowe, archivist, Aberdeen City Archives.Fiona Watson, archivist, Northern Health Board, Aberdeen. Ishbel and Arthur Bennet, Farr. Irene MacKenzie, former head teacher, Dallas School. Molly Douglas, Elgin.Ian Sutherland, Dallas. The late Mary Chalmers, Elgin.The staff at New Register House, Edinburgh. The staff at the National Library of Scotland.Sandy Stewart, Branchill Farm, Dallas. James and Lily MacBean, Gollanfield, Inverness. The staff at the Highland Folk Museum, Kingussie.The staff at MacKenzie and Cruickshank, Forres. Patricia Horne, Oban. Ann Campbell, Balvicar. The late Mr. Dennis MacNeill, former Argyll and Sutherland Highlander and P.O.W. Mr. Roddy MacPherson, former Seaforth Highlander and P.O.W. Mr. Jeremy Inglis, son of Captain John Inglis. Mr. Robert Grieve Black, author of 'Highland Schottische'. Mr.Murdo MacDonald, former Argyll and Bute Archivist. The late Mr. Alasdair Carmichael, former Argyll and Sutherland Highlander and P.O.W. The staff of the Mitchell Library, Glasgow. Mr. Rod MacKenzie, Argyll and Sutherland Highlanders' Museum, Stirling Castle. The Oban Times, in particular Stella McIver. Patrick and Margaret Freytag, Oban, for translations. Rhoda Thomas, Oban, daughter of the late Mr. Archie Gillespie. The Very Revd. Norman MacCallum, Rector of St. John's Episcopal Cathedral, Oban. Lindsay Campbell, Archivist, St. John's Cathedral, Oban. Warner Chappell Music for permission to use the words of "I'll Walk Beside You."
My family for encouragement and support. My dear brother Robbie for photographic expertise. My precious grandsons, Calum

and Finlay, for continuing the family line and bringing such immeasurable joy to us all.

Above all, Ian Hamilton Q.C. for having faith in me.

# Contents

|  |  |  |
|---|---|---|
|  | Biography | v |
|  | Foreword | vii |
|  | Acknowledgements | xi |
| Chapter 1 | Branchill | 3 |
| Chapter 2 | Almost over before it began | 9 |
| Chapter 3 | Loss and Loaf | 13 |
| Chapter 4 | Dallas Days | 19 |
| Chapter 5 | Growing Pains | 26 |
| Chapter 6 | The Promise of the Year | 37 |
| Chapter 7 | Simmer Days | 43 |
| Chapter 8 | Stick Dolls and Burnt Sugar | 52 |
| Chapter 9 | The Pig in the Sidecar | 63 |
| Chapter 10 | The Seventh Day | 70 |
| Chapter 11 | An Education of Sorts | 93 |
| Chapter 12 | Spreading Wings | 102 |
| Chapter 13 | The Turning of the Year | 107 |
| Chapter 14 | Loosening Strings | 116 |
| Chapter 15 | Away Beyond the Green Road | 123 |
| Chapter 16 | Tchaikovsky and Chamberlain | 127 |
| Chapter 17 | Cassocks and Bare Feet | 134 |
| Chapter 18 | Broom Handles and Bad Potatoes. | 139 |
| Chapter 19 | Behind the Wire | 149 |
| Chapter 20 | 'With Ears Like Yours' | 163 |
| Chapter 21 | I'll Walk Beside You. | 172 |
|  | Post Script | 178 |
|  | Sources and Further Reading. | 179 |

# Auld Claes an' Porridge

## Mhairi Livingstone Ross

*Moss-soft and hushed now is the road that leads to Branchill. A road whose cobbles and ruts have been ironed out and polished over years by feet and hooves in the days when folk were at one with the land, coaxing the soil and winning its harvests. Whin and bramble watch over its outgoings and incomings, guarding its secrets and splashing their yellow and purple across the land, according to season. Still, the summer winds, caressing and warm, worry away at the tussocks and the soft rain spills on the earth. And in the winter the far-off growl of the sea can be heard, if you have a mind to hear it, and the touch of the first snows felt, stinging the cheek. And just now and then, voices come to you, canny and kind, echoing from the old place and carried on the wind; voices of bairns laughing or teasing; voices of parents scolding or praising; voices filled with hope or despair.*

# Chapter 1

# Branchill

"Far am ah gyaan, Faither?" I heard my thin voice whisper.

"Wheesht, quinie, dinna fash yersel. Yir jist awa tae Maggie Grant's."

I drowsily half opened my eyes and caught a fleeting glimpse of his face, reassuring and kind, and let his words wash over me. I liked Maggie. That was all right. I closed my eyes again.

Father however looked anxious as he carried me, his youngest daughter, from the house and across the field, green-happit with June corn. Wrapped in a darned blanket plucked in haste from the bed, I was only six and already in the grip of 'the fever' which, yet again, was spreading its malevolence over our community. Before it ran its course it would have claimed two young lives from our small village to add to those who had gone before.

With as much tenderness as his weary arms could impart or custom would allow a man of the soil in 1927, my father carried my slight, febrile body down the rough track from the croft to the stretcher waiting for me at the road end. He handed over his once lively, bright, chatterbox child to the attendants, who placed me in the new motor-ambulance. The last I remembered was the nurse placing a sheet over my face—necessary to prevent infection but terrifying for a child sliding in and out of consciousness and fearfully ominous for my father, powerless to help me more.

Easter Meikle Branchill huddled, as best she could, in the hills above Forres, her back to the Moray Firth and the north wind, soughing and snell, which often in the winter brought snow. Folk had lived there since the days of the Norsemen who named it after the well, pouring out its mineral-rich water high in the hills.

A sister croft, Wester Meikle Branchill, lay across the yard and over the road—Robbie's road—and both were offspring of the mother croft, 'big Branchill', that sat on the crest of the rise above Rafford. They were all on land belonging to Craigmill Estate and were tucked in between Blackhillock to the north and Coldhome, which was set further along the road to Dallas and acted as a buffer for the crofters against the world beyond.

The whole had made a fermtoun in days long gone before improvements, by some folks' way of it, had broken up most of the farming townships into single farmsteads and scattered them amongst newly enclosed fields. Land that had never been settled was given over to individual crofts and that which was poor for the want of good soil and riddled with stones and bog was reclaimed from the clutches of the moor. The old names endured though and, if there were now three crofts where there used to be one, they were styled 'mid' or 'nether', 'easter' or 'wester', 'lower' or 'upper' to distinguish them from their neighbour.

A new strain of village, too, began to replace kirktouns and milltouns of old. A thousand years ago, folk would tell you, this part of Moray had been a favoured spot. A mannie called William de Ripley had been granted land here by William the Lion and later his descendant, Sir William of Dallas, fought on the side of noble King Robert, earning lasting glory for himself by being declared a 'rebel' by Edward Longshanks.

There had been a settlement at Dallas long before Alexander, the 'Wolf of Badenoch,' cut a swathe of terror across the north, sacking and burning Forres and Elgin Cathedral. He had used the ancient dun at Torcastle as his storehouse for the loot plundered on his rampages. The Cummin or Comyn family had received a warrant at the beginning of the fifteenth century to build a castle at Dallas. Their lineage was long and noble, reaching back beyond the bloodied steps of Dumfries Kirk where John Comyn's life was cut short. Their castle had stood at the foot of the Wangie since the early part of the fifteenth century but, with the passage of time, had gradually fallen into disrepair. It was no wonder then that, when the new village was started around 1814, much of the stone, which had formed the thick walls of the keep, was used to build the houses.

The new village consisted of a single street linking Hatton and the Hill of the Wangie to the road to Knockando and Strathspey. The hills of Mulundy, Millbuies, Delnahe, the Meikle Hill and the Wangie surrounded the vale, enveloping it and protecting it from the worst of the weather. By 1839, it boasted around 35 homes arranged in line on either side of a wide road.

The area was well served with grey slate quarries so each dwelling was easily and substantially roofed. Every tenant was able to rent a piece of land behind the house amounting to two Scots acres to grow potatoes and vegetables for themselves and grass and hay to feed their cows. A few scattered dwellings at either end completed the settlement, home to just over a hundred souls. And so it remained for the next four or five generations, old folks dying to make way for the new and each, in their turn, carrying forward the mingled blood of the Celt and Pict and Norseman to become our people. This was the Dallas of my young days—a village so ordinary that you would scarce notice it today but the whole world to the lassie that was I.

From the front door of Branchill, the gentle Moray hills, bare of trees, rolled away as far as you could see over the young, peat-brown Lossie—not quite yet a river—towards the braes of Knockando. From time to time, it would become too swollen to be contained within its banks. Then, it would pour its contents—mineral, vegetable and, occasionally, animal—over the land and wreak havoc and destruction on the neighbourhood.

Flooding was not unusual in our part of the world. As far back as 1097, in the year that Malcolm king of Scotland died, an 'exundation of the German Ocean' was reported to have overwhelmed castles, villages, towns and woods and left the land of Moray desolate. In more recent times, the great spate of 1829 all but destroyed many of the dwellings, crops and much of the livestock in the vale of Dallas. The summer of that year had been excessively hot, worse than folk could remember, and the drought that had come with it had been so extreme that most of the newly planted trees had perished. The 'northern lights' shone brighter and clearer than folk were used to and with them often came a warm wind, stealing over the land and unsettling the beasts in the fields. The first of the rain fell on the coast but very soon the deluge was covering the whole of the land of Strathdearn and Badenoch. A sixth of the usual annual rainfall fell in 24 hours.

'Rain commenced on $2^{nd}$ August and continued 'til the $4^{th}$. A fierce north-east wind stripped the leaves off the trees and whirled them into the air and their thick boughs were bending and cracking beneath the tempest. At the Haugh of Bethlem, the river came so furiously down about 4 o'clock that the house was instantly flooded and the man's wife had no more than time to snatch up her child and run for her life. The fine farm of Craigroy attached to the Mill of Dallas was utterly ruined as to the crop and soil and the river opened a new channel through the finest part of the land. At 4 o'clock in the afternoon, the river burst its left embankment immediately below the narrow pass where it enters the open vale and the whole force of the stream, at a height of over three feet, poured towards the village of 32 houses. Some 120 people had to be evacuated.'

Folk who were there told of the blacksmith, Kenneth MacLean by name, who was very near drowned trying to save his pig. He had stayed behind long after he should have fled to take care of his favourite sow which was about to farrow. As the water rose, his predicament became desperate and he was only saved by his rescuer hauling at his clothes when his head had already been under water for some time. He managed to carry the sow up to his own bed where, we're told, she gave birth to a beautiful litter. No father could have been more proud!

The flood, though disastrous in the havoc it wreaked, threw up some surprises, too. A tenant farmer's wife up at Dalraddy, high in the hills where the Spey is in its infancy, opened her door after the deluge and found, to her amazement, a trout, a pike, a hare, a partridge, a boiling of tatties, a helping of neeps, and one of her own turkeys, ready for the pot! Most of the poor, however, lost all they had—their homes, livestock, land, meal-kist and, for those that had them, their little store of 'picture-books,' the banknotes that had gradually come into their lives.

The Lossie, like most rivers, had plainly not always taken her present course. In the days before men, she had flowed into the loch which covered the valley where the village now stood and out again at Rhininver, flowing through Branchill and into the Black Burn from where she wandered to the sea by way of Briach, Craigmill and Pluscarden. All around the loch was a dense forest, home to wildcat and wolf, elk and bear, wild ox and boar.

We were lucky. The land around our croft was fertile and now far enough away from the vagaries of the new Lossie not to need worry about flooding.

The Laich o' Moray, a thirty mile ribbon five miles at its narrowest, twelve at its broadest, tangled its way round villages and farms, cushioning the land and its folk from the worst advances of the sea and keeping at bay the moors, empty and bleak, to the south.

Sand-blown and lightly textured, the reddish-brown till was stippled and patched with hard Moray pan, coffee in colour and iron, like its folk, in character. For all that, the Laich was well-kent for its farming and husbandry. Trim steadings and clean crops bore testimony to the hard, relentless work and quiet pride of the tenants in their small corner of Scotland's 'cold shoulder', where springs arrive late and autumn frosts come early. Despite a growing season of not much more than two hundred days, Morayshire barley enjoyed a high reputation for quality and was used by the local distilleries that made it their practice to use home-grown over import in making their malt. Water leeching from the Cairngorms was pure and free from minerals and ideally suited for whisky. The mosses on the moors acted as a filter and the peat itself, used for drying the malted barley, enriched the product with its distinctive flavour and aroma.

Over the hill above Branchill lay centuries-old peat-bogs, some deep enough to cover a house, folk would say. Peat-bogs which had their beginnings in the long-gone days when wolves, not men, roamed the place and forests covered the land. Peat-bogs which, every summer, relinquished enough winter fuel to local families who were prepared to make the effort to dig it out.

The peat also provided much needed income for folk who wrested, stacked and carted it to sell to the distilleries round about.

My parents, Robbie and Bella Skene, had been crofters in Branchill since 1910. That year had started well for them. Since their marriage three years before, they had been blessed with first a son and then a daughter, a year later. With her sizeable dowry, Bella Masson, my mother, had brought enough money to the marriage to furnish their new home at Craigroy Mill above the village with a few handsome pieces of furniture and a chest of bonny dishes.

Each year at Whitsun, tenants would be sought to take on the mill and thirty acres of arable and pasture land alongside it. And so in the spring of 1907, Father and his brother William renewed their lease and settled down for another twelvemonth to work the land and mill the meal for the people of Dallas. Father also had the job of public carrier. Each Tuesday was market day in Forres, each Friday in Elgin and Robbie would take himself off with his horse and cart, delivering meal, eggs, cheese and the like to the town and collecting tea, turkeys and tractor parts for the local folk on the way back. He never wrote anything down and always delivered the correct item as well as the exact change. He was highly regarded by all the villagers and they looked forward to his cheery smile and courteous manner. He, in turn, enjoyed the blether and news he picked up along the way. As a wedding gift, the villagers collected thirteen and a half sovereigns to present to him on the eve of his marriage as thanks for his honourable and straightforward dealings in his business with them.

Mother and Father settled into married life at Craigroy, prospered well enough and were able to afford a maid to look after the bairns. Work at the mill was hard and relentless, everyone in the area needing corn milled to provide the staple oatmeal. Time off from the darg was rare. So, when their farmer friend, Sandy, decided to wed the local school teacher, my parents eagerly accepted his invitation to celebrate their marriage in Elgin, leaving young Johnny and his sister, Annie, in the care of their nursemaid.

She couldn't have noticed the toddler wandering off in the late afternoon and she couldn't have heard his infant cries for help or his last, gasping breaths as the water covered his face. When my parents returned from their day out, the maid was beside herself with grief and Johnny's lifeless body lay at the side of the mill-lade.

## Chapter 2

## Almost over before it began

The six miles from the road end at Branchill to Leanchoil hospital in Forres took almost an hour to cover in the new motor-ambulance, a gift from the Red Cross to replace the horse drawn wagon that had come to the end of its useful life. I was oblivious to the sudden jolts, accelerations and cornerings on the uneven road and passed Maggie Grant's without a murmur. I had no recollection of being lifted out of the ambulance and taken into the special fever pavilion at the rear of the hospital. For the next four weeks, I drifted in and out of life, my body's essential requirements being met by way of tube and syringe, bed pan and cooling sponge.

Scarlet Fever is a highly infectious, bacterial disease which, in the 1920's, was a common cause of illness in the country, especially for children. Fever, vomiting and swollen glands in the neck would follow sore head and throat. By the time the tongue started to develop a thick, white coating, it was clear that the infection had taken hold and the patient would be in for a tough time. How tough depended on robustness and general health, but not always. Luck played a part, too.

On the second day of infection, a rash, rough and raised and for all the world like a bad case of sunburn, would appear, spreading its hot and itchy claws first over the neck then the chest and back and slowly covering the rest of the body. After the rash came the peeling—great strips of withered skin sloughing off and leaving, in its place, a new layer, exposed and tender. The fever, bad as it was, also had hidden dangers. Complications were common—rheumatic fever, ear infection, pneumonia, damage to the kidneys and meningitis. Any or all could follow if the patient had not been adequately treated in time of if luck was against them.

My dear friend, also called Molly, contracted the disease several years after I did and minds the anxiety of not only her family but also of the doctor who sat with her all night. She was too ill to be taken to Spynie Hospital in Elgin and was kept in isolation at home. When the fever was at its height, she remembers, in her semi-conscious state, the feeling that she was falling from an aeroplane—tumbling in freefall until, at the last possible moment before she hit the ground, letting out a yell so loud and urgent that she woke up. They told her later that, if she had not cried out, the fever would have claimed her and that would have been that. When she was on the mend, doses of castor oil would be ministered in the belief that purging was good for body and soul. Not too bad though when the taste of it was relieved by a square of chocolate.

I had caught the fever in the infant class at school. A loon staying with his granny in the village had worn clothes sent to him from the town—clothes that had come from an infected house. His granny had sent him to school even though his skin was peeling but had failed to notify the authorities. By the time it became obvious that it was he who had passed on the infection to four other families in the area, he was better.

The youngest Skene daughter, I was nearly six when I had started school. Branchill was almost three miles from Dallas and too far for legs younger than mine to trot there and back. My cousin Maggie, Auntie Nellie's and Uncle John's daughter, had started at the same time and we sat near each other in the infant class. Between us sat the boy who had come from Forres to stay with his granny. Both of us took the fever home.

At Rinavey, just up from Branchill, Uncle John and Auntie Nellie were ill in bed themselves and could do little to help when first Maggie, then young John and finally wee Annie, only three, started to show signs of the illness. By the time Dr. Gibbon the Medical Officer of Health had been notified and taken steps to close the school, the fever had taken a strong hold and, within the space of a week, the Masson loon was in hospital and both of their precious daughters were dead. It fell on my father, being the closest family member unaffected by illness, to lay out the bodies for burial. He never got over the harrowing ordeal of seeing their young, bonny faces blackened by fever, their happy, chattering tongues silent or of having to break the heartbreaking news to their distraught parents.

I had begun to feel unwell on Saturday. By Sunday, I was

feverish and my throat hurt. On Monday morning, Ma shouted to me,

"Time for the school, quinie. Up ye get. Jean an' Meg are doon hivvin' their brose already."

"Ah canna gang the day, Ma, ah've been seek."

"Come awa, noo. Ye'll be fine ance ye've hid something tae eat!"

"Ma, ah'm seek. Ah canna gang the day."

The pain in my throat was making talking very difficult. When my mother came up the stairs to see me, she caught her breath and a ball of fear tightened in her stomach. My neck and face were covered in a fiery rash and the glands in my throat were visibly swollen. Pulling back the bed-clothes, Ma could see the rash had spread over my chest and down my legs. She hurriedly pulled the covers back over me and called for my sister.

"Jean, run tae the village an' get the nurse. Tell her Molly's no weel. Ask her tae come quick!"

It was hard to keep the panic out of her voice and Jean took to her heels. She would have three miles to run to get to the nurse's house and she was barely twelve. It didn't take the nurse long to confirm what my parents already knew and Dr Gibbon was notified. He visited Branchill and completed his report on my condition, the condition of the house and the number of occupants. He confirmed that we had an ash-pit as opposed to a midden, a privy and not a w.c. and that we had their own supply of milk. Information that mattered, I suppose, to some-one. For that, he charged us 2/6d— money my parents could ill afford.

Since the tragedies that had befallen the family over the past years, Ma had not found it easy to cope with illness or difficult situations of any kind. Despite reassurances from the nurse that she wasn't ill, she had convinced herself that she, too, had the fever, and took to her bed. Father had to take over the caring for his sick daughter and prepared a shaky-doon for himself on the floor at the foot of the bed that I shared with my older sisters, Jean and Meg.

In between bouts of vomiting and delirium, I was aware of little except the intense pain in my ears. All night, the pain worsened until I could barely thole it. Father kept my temperature down as best he could with cold compresses but I kept burning up. Suddenly, I sat up in bed and screamed with the stounin' in my ears. An explosion had burst in my head and had started a trickle then a deluge of foul, yellow pus running down my cheeks. My father ran to get wadding—any scraps of cloth he could find—to staunch the flow. The searing pain had at last eased and I slid into a delirious sleep. The following day, the ambulance took me away and my anxious parents, once more, prayed for the life of their child.

# Chapter 3

# Loss and Loaf

Mother and Father couldn't bring themselves to stay at Craigroy after the drowning. They had heard that there was a vacant lease going on a croft at Easter Meikle Branchill, three miles out of the village on the Rafford side. Father had gone to see John Ross at Calhame to see if they would take him on as a tenant farmer. He'd had plenty experience of the work having come from farming stock and serving as a farm labourer at Aulteyuish for George Douglas and shepherd for James Shaw at Knockando. He knew the land well and had reconciled himself to its moods and its pleasures.

They packed their belongings in a cart and, with as much optimism as they could muster, travelled the short distance to their new home.

They loved the place from the first.

Branchill, Brenchill in the tongue o' Moray, with its 'ch ' echoing the loch of the Romach over the hill, was a typical northeast croft house. Her front door welcomed the young family and beckoned them enter a narrow hallway from which they could go in three directions, four if you counted the stairs. To the right was the kitchen, which was to become the heart of the home. On the left, a more formal parlour which, sensibly and without fuss, was called the 'room.' Straight ahead, with its door fitted to lie snugly under the rise of the stair, was Mother and Father's new bedroom. Upstairs, the landing cowered under the sloping roof, laden with its weathered slates and off it two, coom-ceilinged bedrooms, one on either side of the stair-head. Beyond the kitchen, leading out to the back yard, previous tenants had built a porch which gave extra space. Maybe Branchill was not as grand as Craigroy but it would do and Mother and Father set about rebuilding their lives.

Young Annie was thriving in her new home and soon another child would be born. Ma hoped it would be another son. Every man should have a son and was her man not one of the best? He would shape and nurture the loon in his gentle way and they would have a fine laddie to work the croft when they got past being able to tend it themselves.

James Shaw Skene was born on 22$^{nd}$ August and there was no happier couple in the land. Mrs Ross from Calhame had produced thirteen of her own and was deemed well enough acquainted with matters maternal to be trusted with bringing other folks' bairns into the world. Other neighbours, too, came to help with the confinement and assure themselves that all was well with mother and child. Much discussion ensued as to which side of the family he resembled and how he had inherited his father's long, slender hands and his mother's bonny face. Ma, herself, felt relief that her longed-for son had arrived safely and Father—well he just smiled his wise smile and got on with his work. And there was plenty of that.

Water for drinking and cooking had to be carried from the well at the bottom of the garden. Water for washing dirty dishes and clarty hands was kept separate and was drawn from the burn running through the front yard. Pails found a home in the back porch and refilling them daily was a task we were to come to know well over the years. Cows and crops, hens and humans all had to be taken care of and Father worked diligently for them all.

He had all the tatties lifted by early October that year and, as the autumn days slowly gave way to winter in 1911, he considered himself content with his lot. Ma, however, was uneasy. The infant was not thriving and, try as she might, she could not get him to keep his food down. She had plenty milk but the bairn couldn't seem to swallow it. After each feed, he would reject her milk, often forcefully, and then cry pitifully for hours with hunger. By the time she realised that he was not getting enough to nourish him, he was past the point of help. Despite the best efforts of the doctors and nurses at Leanchoil Hospital, her precious son slipped out of this life in the early hours of a cold November morning.

As the summer days lengthened, I slowly improved. Nurses drifted in and out, clad in aprons scrubbed with disinfectant. They still placed cloths on my head to keep my temperature down and gradually I found my appetite again. Light custards and jellies, ice cream and thin soups fed to me by teaspoon slowly built up my strength. My skin had, at last, stopped peeling and my temperature was stabilizing. Each time I woke from the dark place, I found myself in a different room and through the bars of my wee cottie I squinted at my new surroundings. That July day was my seventh birthday and, although still weak and confused, I was impatient to see my family.

Since the fever had come to his door, Father had had a long journey to make every week. His eldest daughter, my sister Annie, although now away from the croft and working at Grangehall in Forres, had caught the infection on a visit home and was a patient in the Joint County Hospital just outside Elgin. Her life hung in the balance for weeks and each time he visited, he would return home with a leaden heart. There seemed to be no bettering for Annie. Each week he would borrow a push-bike and cycle the long road down the Buinach to Elgin, then over to Forres before pedalling back up Rafford Brae and home—a round trip of about forty miles. On the day of my birthday, he had been to see Annie who was still showing no signs of improvement. Worse than that, the doctor had told him that there was now little hope and to go home to prepare his wife for the inevitable. His pale blue eyes, usually so vital and full of fun, were now lifeless. He stood at the window above my cot and, despite his best effort, couldn't summon enough joy even to smile at me.

"Fit's wrang, Faither? Is it Molly? She's a' richt, tell me she's a'richt!"

Young Isabella, who Father aye cried Izey, was my second sister. She was home from her work in Forres to help our parents cope with the youngsters and give Father some help on the croft. She was particularly fond of me and we, despite an age difference of seven years, were very close. We shared the same sense of fun and both of us had inherited our father's sharpness of mind, inquisitiveness and love of learning.

"Och, Izey, Molly's daein' grand but oor Annie's in a bad wye. The doctors dinna hold oot much hope for her. Oh quinie, I canna bear tae lose anither bairn!"

The worry on his face and his obvious distress greatly upset young Bella.

"Ah'll awa an' see them baith, Faither" and, with that she was off, skirts flying behind her, doon Robbie's road on her bike.

Visitors to the isolation ward were allowed to see patients only from outside the window but, even so, I was aye delighted to see any of my family.

"Fa's that at the windae?" I whispered.

"It's me, it's Bella. Fit like are ye the day?"

"Fit are ye sayin'? Ah canna hear fit ye're sayin'."

Bella tried again. She mouthed her greetings through the opening.

"Dinna fash yersel, Molly. Ye've been gey seek this last month and it's guid tae see ye looking weel. Yir lugs will still be sair frae the fever. They'll be fine soon."

"Ah still canna hear ye, Bella. Foo's a'body at hame?"

Bella smiled back and nodded her head.

"They're a' weel an' send their best tae ye. Ah'm off tae see oor Annie noo," and passed a note to me through the window.

When the nurse came round later that day, I was vexed. I had searched everywhere—under the bed, under the bed of the lassie next to me. Michty, I'd even looked in the bath and behind the dresser but couldn't find it.

"Why are you out of bed, Molly? You know you have to rest."

"Ah'm looking for the loaf."

"What loaf would that be, ma dearie?" asked the nurse.

"The loaf Bella brocht. She gave me a notie an' it said there wis a loaf."

"Let me see the note, quinie," replied the nurse softly.

As she read the short message, the nurse looked fondly at her small patient and smiled.

"Bella didn't bring you a loaf, Molly. She brought you something far, far better and much more precious."

I had only had the benefit of a few months' schooling and couldn't yet read well. The note from my sister had ended with 'love, Bella'—no bread, but a special, enduring, indestructible bond that the pair of us would share for the rest of our lives.

The loss of their first-born had all but broken my parents' hearts. The death of their second son stole away much of their spirit, too—especially Ma's.

Isabella Masson was born in 1883, the eldest of five children, to John Masson and his wife, Margaret. Farming was in the blood on both sides and her father reaped the benefit of generations of knowledge and smeddum, lifting himself and his family into a relatively comfortable existence as farmer on the hill of Edinvale, overlooking Dallas. When both he and his wife died of pneumonia within weeks of each other as 1904 dragged to a close, there was enough money from the farm to leave each of the children a sizeable sum to set them up in life.

Bella and her sisters Lizzie and Annie had inherited their mother's high cheekbones and elegant posture. Their father had endowed them with alert, honest, grey-green eyes and fresh complexions. His daughters cut handsome figures and each was, undeniably, a bonny quine. They all benefited from a well-rounded education and were taught dressmaking and piano. They were also expected to do their share of household and farm tasks, though, and visitors would always comment on the fact that poor Bella would be still trachlin' awa long after her sisters had gone off to play. It wasn't that she had more to do than them, it was just, well, she got side-tracked more often than not, what with magazines to read or new kittens to play with. What was the point of exhausting yourself with the dishes if you could have a ride on the binder instead?

Her brother John had followed his father into farming, though the poor man had suffered a serious fall from a hay-stack and injured his back. He didn't like to trouble his folk and hadn't said anything, but, by the time it became obvious that his spine was badly damaged, it was too late to do much about it. He spent the rest of his life with a pronounced hump on his back, which limited his ability to carry out the heavier tasks demanded of a farmer. He lived to be 77 despite his disability, thanks largely to his gentle, industrious, devoted wife, Nellie, who was never more than 4'10" in her stocking soles but who shouldered most of his burdens in life as well as her own.

When her parents died, Bella Masson had moved to the village to be housekeeper to her other brother William. 'Beel' he was to the family and he earned his living supplying peat from the vast bogs around the place to the dozen or so distilleries that had grown up around Elgin. It was while she was living in the village that she met Robbie Skene.

As a loon, Robbie had grown up just outside Dallas at the Cots of Rhininver. His parents, Robert and Anne, had moved there from Elgin where his father had, for a short time, worked as a railway plate-layer. He was now back on the land, the life he knew best, although it paid barely enough to raise his family of three sons and three daughters. Young Robbie was the third born and a very bright scholar. His mastery of numbers and the ease with which he could solve arithmetic problems by converting them to algebra astounded his school masters. He could have gone on to the academy but there was little enough money for the necessities of life never mind schooling. He was to be fee'd to Geordie Douglas up at Aulteyuish as a farm hand and that was that. Folk used to marvel at his slender fingers and artistic hands and wondered if he was best suited for the heavy toil of a farmer but the life befitted Robbie and gave him purpose. He felt at home amongst the hills and was quite content. His marriage to Bella Masson, despite his being ten years older, settled him down and he looked to the future with as much optimism as any man.

I remained in hospital for thirteen weeks, growing steadily stronger and well. As the days of high summer gave way to autumn, the warm wind would blow over the Grampians and the sweet smell of the turned earth would fill the air. My cot would often be taken outside for me to enjoy the good weather and I longed for the day I could get home. As my health returned, so too did the awareness that something was not right with my hearing. If the nurses were speaking to me, face-to-face, I could, by a combination of lip reading and guess-work, decipher what they were saying. If someone turned away or spoke to me from a distance, I could not hear any sound far less fathom what they meant. Give it time, the nurses had said but my parents knew that my hearing had gone and the chances were it wouldn't return. They were overjoyed still to have me given both my cousins had died and any problem with my loss of hearing would be resolved—Father and Mother would see to that.

They were cutting the corn in the high field when I got home. Strange it seemed to me to be back with my sisters and brother after such a long time but no time to think on it—there was a new pig to scrutinise and wonder at. In a few short days, it was as if I had never been away. The only difference now was that, for the most part, my world was noiseless. If Ma or Jean shouted at me, I could just make out what it was they wanted, but for me, the mornings of waking to the song of the blackbird or being soothed by the purring of my kitten or the million other familiar, comfortable sounds that made up my life, were gone forever. The fever had thankfully spared my life but had robbed me of many of the delights of childhood and left me in a silent and often lonely place.

# Chapter 4

# Dallas Days

Mother and Father would go into Forres only occasionally, sometimes together, sometimes alone. From time to time the butcher's van would call and, now and again, Menzies from the village shop would drive round with his mobile shop but, more often than not, messages would be got from the village. This entailed a three-mile walk along the green road if the weather was fine, slightly further along the bottom road if there was snow or it had been raining hard. Ma liked to have a blether with neighbours and villagers that she didn't get the chance to meet very often and, with Father working in the fields all day long, she welcomed any opportunity to escape the confines of the croft for a while. As luck would have it, the day my cousin Jane looked in for a visit, the sun was blazing and Ma used the occasion to take herself off. Young Annie was sleeping quietly in her bed. At two and a half, she still needed naps through the day so Jane seized the chance to catch up with some reading. She installed herself in Father's favourite chair and happily settled down with a cup of tea and a clutch of Woman's Weekly magazines.

Whatever amorous exploits her hero and heroine were entangled in or how many of the twenty two interesting ways to cook rabbit she had conjured up in her mind to give her man for his dinner we don't know but the time passed quickly and it was only when she heard Father coming in for his midday meal that she realised she had never checked on the bairn. Tearing up the stairs with her heart in her mouth she flung open the bedroom door. Annie was not in her bed.

After five years of marriage, Annie was still their only child and had become, naturally, very precious to my parents, if such an emotion could be articulated. Sentiments and feelings were rarely exposed in our part of the world. Jane raced out of the house, Father hard at her heels, and made straight for the burn.

"Please God, let her no be droont— no anither ane."

Thankfully, there was no sign of Annie either there or at the well but there was no sign of her anywhere else either. The pair called and called. No reply and no trace of her whichever way they turned. Perhaps the Rosses at Calhame had seen her.

Father started to run the half-mile up through the fields separating the two steadings but didn't get very far. As he was passing the field where John Ross kept his cattle, something caught his eye. Like a company of stout, slavering sopranos, the cows were standing in a choir round their conductor who was being stroked on the nose by a very small hand.

"Bonnie coo, bonnie coo," cooed Annie, "fit a bonnie coo."

Father was so relieved to have found her safe that he forgot to be angry and made to get through the fence to pick her up. It was only when the coo lifted her head and stepped back that he noticed she had a ring through her nose and her udders were the wrong shape. 'She' was very definitely a 'he' and Annie was sitting only inches from the bull's powerful hooves.

Trying feverishly to keep calm but knowing the beast could turn on her at any minute, Father spoke softly to his child, coaxing her with the promise of tasty titbits and special treats rather than the leathering he felt like giving her for causing him so much anguish. Whatever the delicacy was that appealed to her, Annie decided she'd had enough of the bonnie coo and crawled back under the fence into the arms of her very relieved father.

It would not be the last time she went exploring on her own nor would it be the end of Father's worries but for now he was only too glad he would not have to break more tragic news to his wife.

In the days before the first war, families in the country were seldom planned. Rather, they happened along as God, opportunity or lust ordained. And so it was with us. By the end of harvest time, Ma knew that there was another child on the way—another birth to endure and another life to pray for and worry over. All her pregnancies had been straightforward and she had no reason to doubt this one would be. You just got on with it and took what came your way and if the bairn survived you were pleased; if it didn't, there would aye be anither.

Winter had been mild that year and Father had all his dreels turned early. By April, the tatties had been planted, the corn was sown and he was well under way with the neeps. He would come home after his toil and sit himself down in his chair by the fire while Ma would busy herself making his supper. Porridge it would be usually. Sometimes he would get a boiled egg and oatcakes to go with it, sometimes not. The diet was monotonous and predictable. Bread and jam would fill corners that were left empty by the paucity of the meals but were no substitute for nourishment. Despite that, Father always found enough energy to see that his work was done.

    Annie was now three and as inquisitive about life as any other toddler. She would wander off to blether with Jane Cameron across the way and even had been found up at Rinavey at Auntie Nellie's, a good half mile away. She had been warned time and time again about keeping away from the burn and, so far, had heeded the warnings. But that evening in April, with her mother a month away from her next confinement, Annie was missing again. Father tried all the usual places but, as the spring light faded in the sky, there was still no trace of her. He felt the familiar coldness of fear creep over his heart but tried to dismiss it as he ran for his neighbours to help with the search. Auntie Annie from Elgin stayed with Ma, who was beginning to feel the well-known discomfort in her lower back. The Rosses from Calhame joined the Camerons and Uncle John, Auntie Nellie's man, and they spread out, searching every corner of every field, under every pile of straw and in behind every dyke and bush. Father tore at the heather on the rough ground and dismantled the remains of his peat stack with his calloused hands but could find no trace of his daughter. It was well past midnight and their neighbours, by this time as anxious and distraught as themselves, convinced each other to go home to see to their own families before returning at first light to carry on with the search. Ma's pains were now coming every ten minutes or so and she knew it wouldn't belong before the bairn would come.

    As the first rays of light bleached the sky, Father, white-faced and bleery, pulled on his boots to start the hunt again. A scuffle at the back door made him lift his head just enough to catch sight of his sleepy, straw-studded child, toddling towards him, clutching a cloth.

    "Oh, Annie, far hiv ye been? We've a' been searchin' aawye for ye."

He gathered her up in his arms and stroked her soft hair tenderly. Worry evaporated and gave way to relief as he held her tightly against his chest.

"Ah wis in the fald wi' the caafies in ma wee hoosie unner the cairt. Can ah hiv some brose, faither, ah'm gey hungry? Far's Ma?"

Poor Ma was well into labour by now and, between pains, was at least comforted by the news that Annie had been found. This bairn was not meant to arrive for another month but with all the worry over Annie it wasn't going to wait. Ma herself wasn't showing much and didn't expect the child to be very big. When she eventually appeared, however, Isabella Skene was no bigger than a two-pound bag of sugar. Auntie Annie was with Ma for the confinement.

"That thing will never live!" she uttered more out of despair than malice and poor Ma turned her head to the wall. After her long travail, it was not the news that she wanted to hear.

'That thing', my dearest sister Bella, did live, however, a fighter from the start and throughout her long life was and still is one of the most remarkable, resourceful and resilient women of her generation—a generation that, in these parts certainly, produced many remarkable women.

1914 opened in Dallas with a celebration of the coming of age of James, the son of the Houldsworth family, owners of Dallas Estate. All the tenantry were invited and were well fed and watered. Spoken with genuine warmth and sincerity, the speeches praised the mettle of the tenants and acknowledged their 'fine old-world spirit of loyalty and devotion to the lord of the manor.' There followed entertainment by conjurer and ventriloquist and the evening was rounded off by the traditional dance—a gesture of kindness in providing simple pleasures for folk who seldom got the opportunity to go to the town and whose life was largely governed by weather and work and worry.

Dallas estate had been acquired in 1908 from Sir William Cumming whose family had held it for generations. The Lodge itself, originally called Rhininver House, had been built by Sir Robert Gordon and was intended as a replica of his home at Gordonstoun but was never completed. Instead, only a semi-circle of outbuildings and offices were finished but the overall layout proved to be more attractive than the original and it was left like that.

Even as the Austro-Hungarian Empire was disintegrating and events in Europe were moving ominously towards war, Father, Ma and their two young daughters settled into the gentle rhythm of the seasons—the ploughing, drilling, planting, hoeing and harvesting which regulated their lives and those of their neighbours. The lights may have gone out all over the rest of Europe but in his wee corner of the land, Father kept his double-wick lamp aglow. Despite the toll of death growing in Flanders, the poppies still tossed their heads in the breezes over Branchill and summer still wove its vivid tapestry over the land, quilting it cornflower blue, poppy red and marigold yellow. Broom and whin, heather and rowan conspired together to turn the often bleak hills into a commotion of colour from May till September.

Before the days of instant entertainment, the Fornicht was regarded as quite a special occasion by the people of Dallas and surrounding district, though I'm sure something like it would have been enjoyed throughout most country places in the hours between supper and bed. Every week or so, folk would gather in an appointed house to discuss the news of the nation and add their individual slant on events.

Once the world had been put to rights, amusements in the form of cards or draughts would follow, no doubt accompanied by a dram or two for the men and a lemonade for the ladies. The Fornichter often used the occasion to court his neighbour's daughter and it was common practice to start an impromptu dance in the biggest room or barn if a fiddler was amongst those present. The evening was spent in 'harmony and good feeling' and helped to cement together the scattered community in the days before telephone and easy travel made such events less frequent.

The war in Europe was a world away from the daily darg in Branchill but from time to time word would filter through as to what was happening. Newspapers carried weekly bulletins of those who had lost their lives, had been wounded or were missing and good souls like Mrs MacKessack from Ardgye would offer her services as receiver of clothing for destitute Belgians. All were urged to 'save for Tommy.'

As the war dragged on, more names were added daily to the obscene death toll. By the beginning of 1917, when the Roll of Honour was called out for the county of Moray, name by glorious name, those who had gone to war and were lost in the trenches and mud of the Somme numbered eighty-four souls. From Dallas and district alone, thirty-eight names were inscribed on the War Memorial that was erected at the crossroads in the village.

During these troubled years, two more bairns were born to our family—Jane Cameron in 1915, called after our neighbour at the time, and Margaret, named for Father's sister, Maggie, three months before swords were turned back into ploughshares and hostilities ceased. Over the years, Jane became Jean and Margaret was shortened to Meg.

For all bairns, the lives of adults and their conversations are made all the more interesting if only hinted at or spoken of in hushed tones. Wee lugs would strain to make sense of salacious tit-bits or try to fathom grains of gossip that maligned a neighbour or put a perceived wrong-doer in his or her place. It wasn't meant maliciously, not always anyway, and the very same sinner would usually be brought back into the fold of respectability next week when it was some other poor soul's misfortune to have strayed from the straight and accepted narrow.

Annie couldn't have been more than four or five when the Women's Guild held one of their meetings in 'the room' in Branchill. Each member would have the honour of playing host to the others each month, allowing the opportunity for neighbours and friends to visit each other for a blether and a good look. Most likely they admired Ma's bottomless copper jug and the fine china ornaments adorning the whatnot in the corner. The fire in the room would be lit and the peat might even be supplemented with coal from the beautiful, inlaid, wooden box, which, for most of the year, lay unused on the hearth. Ma would get a chance to show off her lovely rosewood table, if only for a short time. In fact, 'the room' was only ever used for Guild meetings or if the minister happened by and we bairns were seldom allowed in. We got to play games with the other children in the kitchen as long as we behaved ourselves.

For Ma, who had started her married life in comparative wealth, now, because of circumstance, struggled to make ends meet, these evenings in 'the room' represented the life she could have had and she savoured the few occasions she could enjoy her parlour until the harsh reality of her life came knocking again at the door.

Either Ma didn't notice Annie sitting quietly in the corner or she didn't realise that her eldest was devouring the gossip every bit as much as the fairy cakes.

As the last of the Guild set off for home, Annie helped Ma tidy up and return the room to its usual formality. When the solitary picture on the wall, urging the 'Kindly Light' to Lead, was adjusted and the paraffin lamp extinguished, Annie's small voice was heard to lisp,

"Aye, that Lizzie his a face like a soo's backside that's never seen the sun."

If you can imagine the deep red of rowan berries or the beaming glow from a ripened tomato, then you'll have some idea of the colour of Ma's face. Not for the first time, she was glad the darkness hid her blushes as she quickly ushered her young daughter up the stairs to bed. She resolved to be more discrete with her observations in future.

# Chapter 5

# Growing Pains

With their family growing, Father and Mother relied more and more on Annie and young Bella to help with farm and household chores. The girls, both now at school, worked hard at their lessons and even harder when they came home. When they did find time to play it would often be at wee hoosies. Any suitable stone or broken bit of glass would become a wall, window or door and imagination would do the rest. Bella's hoosie would always have a bathroom—the very pinnacle of aspiration to a small child whose world was simple and often without material wealth. She didn't know that she was poor. Everyone else in her ken was much the same as herself, though some quines like our cousin Margaret seemed to have more than one jersey and even had shoes in the summertime.

Even at an early age, Bella knew that she had two tongues—one, the speak of the farming folk for home and family and the other, more formal, for school and the minister. They were kept separate, neither one challenging or tarnishing the other. On the day her sister Annie had had an accident with the boiling water from the kettle, Bella phrased and re-phrased her apology for missing school as she ran along the green road in diction she deemed suitable for the cultured ears of the teacher. To her credit, Miss MacDonald's jaw didn't as much as twitch when it was explained that Annie had 'birned her fowt on the kattle' and the explanation for her absence was accepted and received with as much sympathy as was appropriate.

When Mr. Crawford succeeded Mr. Izatt as headmaster, he brought to Dallas School compassion and empathy for his pupils as well as a love for learning. Some said it was because he came from farming stock himself and that he understood the toil and sacrifices ordinary folk made for their bairns' education. On the day that Father needed Bella to stay and help with the hoeing of the neeps, he sent her first to 'run over' to the school to ask the master's permission.

"The hoe, Bella, are you sure it's the hoe you're wanted for? I hear there's a circus on in Forres. Are you sure you're not off there?"

"Oh no, Sir, we couldn't afford to go to the circus. My father needs me to help him with the hoe."

She got her permission to miss school and ran back along the green road.

The following Saturday afternoon, one of the few cars in the area stopped at our road end and Mr. Crawford got out. Spying Robbie in the field, he called to him and the two exchanged a few words.

"Get yir coat, Izey, and be quick aboot it. Mr Crawford canna wait all day."

Bella did as she was bid and ran to the car. Inside were the two other senior pupils of the school. For children who had little money and enjoyed few treats, the excitement of a trip in a car, never mind a visit to the circus—a selfless gesture from a kind headmaster—would remain with them long after they had left school behind and entered another world where generous acts were rare and looking after self often replaced consideration for others. When, some months after she had left the school, Bella met him in the village, he looked at her fondly and said,

"Aye, aye, Bella, I had high hopes for you. You could have done well at the academy, given the chance."

But the chance couldn't be given. Bella knew it and, in his heart, Mr. Crawford knew it too.

Harvest time was always a time for relief amongst the farmers and crofters, especially if the rains had kept off and the yield had been good. Once safely gathered, folk could relax a bittie and catch up with each other's news. There was still a warmth in the evening air and the full moon, hanging yellow and ponderous, poured out its light like a river of gold coursing over the hills from heaven. On such a night, love was for the making and the taking and mony a bairn was started in the days and nights that followed the hairst, as summer slipped imperceptibly into autumn.

I was born on 21$^{st}$July, 1920, the fifth and last daughter to the

Skenes. I was to be called after Ma's sister but it wasn't easy to decide what form of the name I should have. Lizzie was fine and so was Molly.

"Mak up yir mind fit tae cry her and be done wi't," Father would mutter from behind his paper but Ma would dither and swither until her man could stand it no longer.

"Her name's to be Molly and that's an end tae it."

And Molly it was.

Right from the first, I was interested in what was going on. My eyes would follow any movement across the room and light up like stars when my sisters took their turn of rocking the cradle or singing to me. As I grew, it was obvious I had inherited my father's love of learning and would chatter constantly at his side as he tried to snatch five-minutes peace reading The Northern Scot, deeving him with my questions but secretly pleasing him that I took such an interest in my world and his.

As infant days passed and my scope for exploration widened, I would often toddle over to Annie Mac's or totter up the farm road to Auntie Nellie's place to play with my cousin Maggie who was just two months older than I was. The family would often have folk dropping by. Neighbours would call in for a blether and the occasional relative would happen along if they were in the area. The day the mole-catcher called, I was playing at my mother's feet, quietly amusing myself with some distraction or other.

Moles were plentiful around Branchill and their skins could fetch 120/- per hundred, if the adverts in the paper could be trusted. The mole manny would catch and skin the moles and hang the pelts to dry on the long fence at the side of the house. He was a regular visitor and Father enjoyed his company. As he rose to his feet, he put his cup down, looked over to me and lifted his sack.

"Ah, weel, ah'll just put her in ma baggie an' be off."

I was on my feet and half way under my parents' bed next door before the mole-catcher had time to reassure me that he was pulling my leg. Such was my alarm that I stayed put till long after I had heard his footsteps echoing off the stone floor and the door closing behind him. It was to be one of the few memories I would have of being able to hear, fixed in my mind by infant terror.

It would be about this time that my parents produced their final contribution to the Morayshire population. Alexander arrived in May 1925, finishing off their family, as they had started, with a boy. Sandy he became and grew up very much loved by his parents and sisters.

The Great War changed much in Morayshire as elsewhere and, when it ended, life was never to be the same again. The loss of life of many of its young men altered the pattern of living, marrying and reproducing that had existed for generations. Changes from horse to tractor also resulted in a dramatic reduction in the number of farm servants and, between the two, the population fell by an eighth in the 1920's.

Dallas was, however, still well served with shops. As well as Menzies grocery shop, there was Willie Sutherland's general store that also baked its own bread and produced the most succulent softies and currant loaves I've ever tasted. We had a post office, smithy and carpenter, a tailor and cobbler, a meal mill, sawmill and woollen mill. Meat and bread vans regularly supplied their produce to those unable to get into the shop. There also existed two churches—the Church of Scotland and the United Free Church, to which our family adhered. It was situated on the hillside at Hatton, at the junction of the Dallas road end with the Forres-Elgin road.

A Women's Guild was in place and, in 1921, the Houldsworth Institute opened, providing a much needed meeting place and centre for the community.

In thanksgiving for the safe return from the war of their sons and other Dallas men, James and Mrs. Hamilton Houldsworth, owners of Dallas Estate, had erected in the centre of the main street a handsome building which housed a library, reading room, recreation room and main hall as well as kitchen and dressing rooms. It was a much needed and much appreciated gathering place provided for a community with little in the way of material wealth but rich beyond words in the respect and consideration they had for each other, owner or orraman, gentry or gamekeeper.

Jean was Ma's favourite, so she said, not because she necessarily possessed qualities the others didn't, but because, according to Ma, she had given her the least trouble as a bairn. She would lie quietly while the foot rocked the cradle and the hands knitted a measured length of sock. As she grew, she would display many of Ma's own characteristics and shared her docile and languid nature.

Whatever perceived injustice it was that ruffled her feathers that afternoon, Jean felt compelled to clype on Bella to Ma. No doubt

Bella, in turn, felt chastened after her punishment—most likely a clout round the ears—but the hot burning of her lugs was nothing to the red rage of vengeance boiling up in her belly.

"Fit aboot a swing, Jean? Wid ye like me tae gie ye a pushie?"

Jean nodded and off the two ran into the barn where two sturdy ropes, yoked together with a plank from an old fish box, dangled from the central rafter. The wooden seat had been well used over the years and had achieved a high degree of polish from a succession of local backsides. Jean gripped the ropes and wriggled her seat into the most comfortable position she could.

At first all went well—Bella pushing and Jean cawing awa like onything. Just as she was beginning to feel she'd had enough swinging, Bella suggested a birl. Jean held fast as Bella started winding the ropes round each other. The twist grew tighter and tighter and climbed higher and higher until it almost reached the roof of the barn. Then Bella stopped. She paused. Then she let go.

"That'll larn ye tae clype tae Ma!" muttered Bella under her breath and scooted off, leaving Jean birlin like a peerie.

Of course, as the twist unwound one way, it tightened the other and, for what seemed like an eternity, Jean held on terrified to let go. When she eventually reckoned Jean would have learned her lesson, Bella crept back into the barn to find her sister flat out on the floor. Revenge quickly gave way to anxiety.

"Jean, Jean, are ye all richt? Speak to me, Jean, wake up, wake up!"

Eventually, with much heaving and tugging, Bella got her sister to her feet and the two started off across the yard, reeling and stotting like a loon lurching homeward after his first night on the beer. Ashen of face, shoogly of leg and most certainly heaving of stomach, Jean tried her best to regain her balance. It must have been a particularly good meal she'd had that day because, just as Ma's feet appeared on the back step, so did the copious contents of Jean's stomach, splattering the door—and the walls—and most of Ma's skirt!

If Bella's ears had hurt before, her backside could have roasted a herring that night.

"This'll— SKELP— larn ye—SKELP—no tae—SKELP—mak yer—SKELP—sister—SKELP—seek—SKELP, SKELP, SKELP."

Despite her throbbing rear and wounded pride, Bella spent most of the night checking that Jean was still breathing, while Jean, with all the smugness of the self-righteous, slept on, only now and again opening one eye to catch sight of her sister tip-toeing out through the door.

Jean didn't much like school and tried every way she could to avoid going. Bella and the others frequently had to resort to abduction and did their best at constraining her by one means or another until she could be bundled into the barrow. This they would try to manoeuvre between gateposts and fences until the Rosses' field was reached and the going was less tortuous. Progress was usually slow, with the wheel often becoming embedded in the mud. The prospect of being late for school usually put paid to their endeavours and Jean would be tipped unceremoniously on the ground to make her own way to school or back home, as she pleased. It usually pleased her to go home where the others would find her behind a dyke or propped up against a stook, having a quiet time.

If Jean was docile and easy-going, Meg was even more so. She was the quietest one in the family, always preferring to keep to herself and finding company amongst the heroes of any book or magazine she could find. She would take herself off to secret places with a book and the rest would have a devil of a job finding her if she didn't want to be found. She rarely wanted to join in with the more boisterous exploits of her sisters, which was understandable given that her nature was douce and quiet as much as theirs was adventurous and wild.

One of the many jobs to be done about the place was the feeding of any calves and it was a job Bella enjoyed. In fact, she much preferred mucking out the byre and working in the fields to being stuck inside doing housework. A newly born calf always got the first of its mother's milk—what we called boosht—which looked and tasted like egg custard. After that, if the cows were not milked thoroughly by hand, their milk would dry up so the calves were often fed their mother's milk from a pail and the rest used for butter, cheese and cream as well as providing us with our staple drink. We drank gallons of milk and in later years, were very grateful for our high calcium levels. Not one of us ever developed osteoporosis or broke a bone.

One particular day, Bella was feeding a new grey calf, smelling its sweet newborn smell and snuggling beside it in the fald—the fold where all the new calves were housed until they were deemed strong enough to join the outside world. Feeding over, she stepped back and plunged her foot into the jaws of an upturned broken bottle, long discarded but still sharp. The glass ripped at her ankle, severing the tendons, nerves and tearing much of the muscle.

Sympathy was something only dispensed if you were at death's door so Bella never thought to mention it to Ma. She wrapped the wound as best she could and didn't make a fuss. It was days later when Ma noticed the blood and swelling that the extent of the injury was realised. Jimmy Ross at Calhame had a pony and trap and was only too happy to take Bella down to Forres to see Dr. Beaton. Because of the length of time that had elapsed since the accident, the body had started its own healing and by the time the doctor could do his job, it was impossible to repair the ankle to its normal working state. Nevertheless, it had to be stitched and he set about the task without anaesthetic or any form of analgesic. When Bella emerged from the surgery, white-faced and trembling, Jimmy Ross remarked,

"Michty, Bella, you've certainly got a guid pair o' lungs. They could hear yon screams in Elgin!"

"I'd like tae see you daein' ony better, Jimmy Ross, wi' bits o' yir banes stickin' oot an' a doctor mannie sewing ye back thegither with naething tae soothe the pain!" Bella retorted between sobs.

Even as a youngster she had an answer for everything.

Annie had already left school and home when I first trotted through the doors of Dallas Public School. She found employment firstly at Hillockhead and then at Grangehall in Forres as a domestic assistant and would only be home on days off or holidays from then on. When Bella reached fourteen, she was off too to help Auntie Annie in Forres. Each time the girls came back, whether it was for a night or a week, the question would always be the same,

"Are ye hame tae bide?"

I missed them sorely when they left.

Auntie Annie was Ma's youngest sister and had married Alex Fraser, the butcher. They lived at Leys Cottage, which, despite its name, was quite a sizeable dwelling on our terms. Uncle Alex was blind and Bella's first job of the day was to rise at five-thirty and help him into the shop to set up the slicing machines for the day. As well as being his eyes, she had to anticipate potential hazards for a blind man working with sharp machinery, which I imagine were plenty. But, for Bella, there were other dangers in the butcher's shop, too.

One of the young lads who worked in the back shop making sausage meat either had taken a shine to Bella or thought he would try her with his charm. An innocent from the croft, she thought he was being friendly until his hands started wandering up her skirt. As quick as you like, she turned on him, clutching a basin of boiling water.

"If ye ever do that again, I'll throw this ower ye. That'll soon stop ye in yir tracks, ma mannie!"

Bella, like the rest of us, had to grow up fast in the world of work and learned the harsh truth that not everyone was as well disposed to her as her own folk had been.

I have no recollection of my first day at school but it was officially recorded that my father enrolled me on 20$^{th}$ April 1926, just three months short of my sixth birthday, so that must have been that.

There were three classes in Dallas School in these days. Miss MacDonald subdued the infant classes—children rounded up after the appointed birthday and contained in alien surroundings until they conformed to what was regarded as acceptable behaviour. Her predecessor was a warm, motherly woman who always referred to her charges as her 'babies'. And to her, in the days when, on marriage, women were forced to give up their careers in the classroom, they probably were a substitute for a family of her own. All was not as it should have been, however. There were strange happenings in her classroom.

Every so often, she would disappear into the cupboard in the classroom that, everyone assumed, housed books, paper and the like. A strange pattering noise would then be heard, accompanied most certainly by discreet coughing or foot shuffling. After a few minutes she would emerge and resume lessons. It was only when one of the senior pupils was sent to her room by the headmaster on some errand or other, that the teacher in question was found in the cupboard, on her chantie, performing a bodily function normally reserved for the water closet outside—much to the surprise and embarrassment of the loon, who had never even harboured the notion that a teacher might need to 'go' during class time. The practice was not surprisingly discontinued after that and the infant mistress had to learn to control her bladder, like every one else, until the bell rang.

In any infant class, then as now, there comes to the nose a rich mixture of smells. In my early days in school, a faint aroma of chalk, cocoa, ammonia and peat-smoke pervaded the air, often fused with body odours of varying strengths and origins. In the days before daily baths, showers and washing machines, the smell of the land came through our clothes and our skin. We were all the same and nobody minded. At least, we children didn't mind. Maybe the teachers did but they, in their wisdom, knew better than to object.

The infant classroom was arranged in tiers with us sitting three to a desk. The blackboard was fixed securely to the wall and a partition ensured that we were not exposed to the mysteries of the middle class before we were thought ready. The walls were always painted a cheerful yellow, probably in an attempt to bring a little sunshine into our world—or perhaps the authorities had a surplus of that shade of paint. Either way it brightened up our surroundings and, with one or two interesting pictures of the 'cocoa pickers in Ghana' variety and maps of the world splashed in pink, the walls of our term time home embraced us with a feeling of security and structure that made learning easy.

Slates with wooden frames were provided along with slate pencils, screeching and skraichin', as endless, repetitive copying ensued until alphabet and numbers were reproduced to the satisfaction of the teacher. We learned our vowels mechanically from the Beginner's Playway and Beacon Infant Readers illuminated our path with worthy legends such as:

'See me, mother
Can you see me?
I can see you
I can see Kitty.
Can you see Rover?'

I suppose every infant has his Kitty and Rover to bear!

Jean must have decided that she would get herself to school that particular day, but as events turned out, probably wished she hadn't. For some reason, Miss MacDonald was not in her usual place and I, along with the rest of my infant cohort, had to go into the senior class where Jean sat, trying to keep as inconspicuous as possible. That was not possible having me as her sister and I waved a cheery hello. It was all very well teaching me to copy letters and numbers but no one had thought to tell me how to wipe them off. Most of my classmates had jaloused that, in the absence of a cloth, the sleeve of a jumper would do. I was more pragmatic and didn't see any reason for getting my jersey dirty. When the time came for our slates to be cleaned, I held mine up to my face and began licking the scribbles and scrawls off. I gradually became aware of tittering from Primary Six, two boys who sat near the back of the classroom and, when I raised my head, realised no-one else had employed that particular method. Looking over at Jean, I could see that she was scarlet from crown to collar and later in the playground, she denied all knowledge of me, despite the fact that we were the only family named Skene in the school and everyone knew we were sisters anyway.

The monotony of the classroom would occasionally be broken by the arrival of a workman as, with the building growing older, doors and windows had to be replaced at regular intervals. No opportunity could ever be missed to lighten the mood and inject some fun into our humdrum day. We were chanting our spelling words as the joiner was fitting a new window in our classroom.

'U-P—up, U-P—up,
G-O—go, G-O—go,
Gie's a bit o' putty, Joe,
G-O—go, G-O—go.'

The teacher must have been distracted for she never noticed, or, if she did, was so impressed by our inventiveness and daring that she let it go without comment.

We went bare foot from April till October until the authorities, in their wisdom, decreed that the practice should cease. The soles of our feet, from time to time, were inevitably punctured by sharp stones, broken glass, corners of farming implements and ends of fencing wire half buried in the grass. For all that, our feet were as tough as leather and nothing then or since, can match the thrill of grass, fresh with dew on an early spring morning, whipping bare legs or running along the green road in summer with warm mud, often suffused with sharn, oozing between toes.

Winter was a different matter. Money had to be found to buy boots for us all from MacIntosh's Boot Warehouse in Forres, although, more often than not, I inherited Jean's, Meg's or even my cousin Margaret's cast-offs. Bella soon learned that the best way to keep hers looking newly polished was to dip them in the burn at the end of the green roadie before going into school.

Nearest in age, Meg would accompany me to school and we would either sprint or meander along the green roadie, depending on time, curiosity or level of hunger. We were aye hungry and the pieces we had brought for our dinner would be eaten well before we got to school. We ate anything we could find to fill our bellies—rasps in July, blaeberries in August, brambles in September and of course, neeps. It wasn't really stealing if the fermer had plenty and you were only eight and had a belly like a torn blanket. You would, of course never take one from your neighbour's field but make sure you were well out of sight of home before choosing a suitable victim from the straight dreels. Many's a time, the farmers along the green road must have scratched their perplexed heads as, every now and again, stones were harvested instead of neeps—stones carefully chosen to fit the hole where the young vegetable once grew. If they had looked a bit closer they might have discovered tell tale clues as to the fate of their crops—tops and tails and discarded skin with infant teeth marks betraying the culprits. My, but these neeps tasted sweet to a hungry child—all the more so by the manner of their getting. In all truth, it's likely those farmers didn't mind too much. If their cattle were short of one or two neeps that winter, at least a neighbour's bairn hadn't gone hungry to school.

## Chapter 6

## The Promise of the Year

On spring mornings, running along the green road was a delight if time could be taken to savour it. The stones, moss-green on the dyke, told of folk long dead, and their toil, endless and raw, for the winning of the land against the hard weather and the talons of moorland, clawing and grasping to keep hold.

The crofts had not always been there. When folk first came to these parts, they had to set about clearing the land and building a home for themselves—some like Corrie Willie Grigor up at Clashdon living in a hole in a bank with his wife and family 'til the job was done.

The burn ran along the length of the road, which was not a road at all but a grassy or muddy track, depending on the time of year and the severity of the weather. Pools arranged themselves along the burn like a collection of secrets, hiding treasures for the finding. Frogspawn, like grey tapioca, trembled with burgeoning life and the occasional minnow would dart or meander by.

Blackbird and thrush accompanied our laughing and singing and, over the fields, came the frantic cry of the peewits, defending their nests with such determination that I marvelled at the nature of them being such good parents to their brood, an all. I would, just now and then, give thought to my own parents and kent fine they, too, would fight to the death for me and the others. Though they didna often give cuddles or the like, we knew we were loved and we in turn loved them without question. Ma did the cloutin' if punishment was needed but she was kind in her own way too, taking other fowks' bairns in if things were hard for them at hame and trying her best with the little she had.

Spring was the time for Father to turn the earth again in readiness for planting. With the gulls chorusing behind him, he would yoke Love our mare to the plough and set off on the well-kent path to coax another yield from the soil. The fields would be used, in turn, for corn, tatties and neeps, with one field always left fallow. All the cattle and horse manure was forked out of the fald and we would spread it as evenly as we could over the fields that needed it. It was great stuff, manure. Bella still swears it makes a grand poultice for drawing skelves and poison to the surface of a wound.

"It's so strong, it'll even draw teeth," she's aye fond of saying, though she's never convinced me that she's tried it for toothache!

If Father ever found a peewit's nest as he was ploughing, he would stop and carefully lift it, scant though it was, to one side, returning it to its original home when he had finished. We would set the dry whins alight every spring to encourage new growth and revelled in the power of fire to destroy while, at the same time, nourish new life.

When corn was to be planted, Father would scatter lime from a canvas bag suspended over his neck by a leather harness, broadcasting it as far to the left and right as he could manage. The rain would wash it in to fertilise the soil and hopefully ensure a good crop.

The chain harrower would be brought out next and Love would pull the wide-toothed rake, scouring all the land of stones and pulling them to the end of the dreels at the top of the field near the house. The hopper, filled with corn seed, would then be pulled up and down the dreels, releasing just enough grain to ensure an even spread and finally a metal roller would be dragged over the field to consolidate the seed bed and flatten the ground in readiness for harvesting. A scarecrow would be fashioned out of any old rags that could be spared, in an attempt to protect as much of the seed as possible and there he would stand, bedraggled and alone, as he watched over our fields and our family.

Tatties would be planted in another field after the grubber had cleared the weeds and manure had been spread. I would often help with the planting, dropping a seed potato into the dreel every foot space. We had Kerr's Pinks, Edzell Blues and Forty Folds and enjoyed them all. Later in spring was the time we prepared the ground and planted our neeps. The field had to be manured and ploughed to give ridges of a suitable depth for the turnips to be easily thinned and weeded. Our horse-drawn two-drill sower was yoked to Love and I would contentedly follow behind, opening and shutting the seed boxes as instructed by Father. As they grew, the neeps had to be thinned with the hoe and we often were called on to help. It was a wearisome task, I can tell you, up and down these dreels scraping and bending and lifting to allow the neeps room to swell.

What a grand working beast Love was. Without her, Father's tasks would have been impossible. We treated her well mind you, aware of our need to keep her strong for the work we asked her to do. I mind the day poor Love slipped and broke her leg. She had to be shot and I know it almost broke my father's heart to do it. She had been his faithful and uncomplaining companion for many ploughings and harvests, sharing his good times and bad and keeping secret his hopes and fears. When she died, we got another mare, Kate, who was an ex-service horse, and still had her army number tattooed on her neck.

Spring also meant a break from lessons. Easter was celebrated at Church with the annual stories of the last supper, the crucifixion and the empty tomb. We celebrated in our own way by boiling some of Ma's precious eggs with either tea or docken leaves to give them a bonny colour and drawing faces on them. Meg, Jean, Sandy and I would then climb the hill at the back of the house and roll them again and again until they cracked. We didn't get eggs often and I mind how much we enjoyed the taste of them, despite the bits of grass, moss and usually sharn that stuck to them.

Hame was always a good place to come back to after school. Ma would aye have a list of jobs for us to do but for the most part, we didn't mind. It was the same for everyone and we just got on with it. Two water pails would have to be filled each day from the well to be used for drinking and cooking. Water for dishes and other washing could be got from the burn which ran past the house, purling and tinkling on its way to the sea. These were kept in the back porch outside the kitchen door.

Milk from our two cows was left to settle in jugs and basins—some to be used for butter, some for cheese but mostly to be drunk by us bairns who were aye thirsty. Most of the butter and cheese would be sold to pay for the growing demands of our growing family.

The fire in the kitchen was just a big hole in the wall at the foot of the chimney, banked up on two sides by binkies—whitened bricks used as hobs for resting pots and kettles that were always at the ready. The swey swivelled over the fire and pots hung on it could be swung round to dangle at just the right height over the peat fire when porridge was needed. Ma would make oatcakes, bannocks or scones as the fancy took her. There was no oven in which to bake so everything was cooked on the open fire, either in the big, black pot, which had to be decoked regularly, or on the griddle iron, which could be settled on the peats. Soot from the lum always found its way into our food—it didn't seem necessary to pick it out and it took me many years to get used to eating porridge that wasn't peppered with black.

I would like to be able to say that Ma was a good cook, but in all honesty I can't. The heart had gone out of her and every day seemed to weary her more. Each Saturday afternoon, the butcher's van from Forres would call on its rounds. Serving Rafford, Dallas and Kellas and all the farms and crofts in between, it would stop at our road end and invariably we would get a bit of boiling beef for soup in exchange for a rabbit. How the butcher kept our and, no doubt, our neighbours' rabbits fresh till Monday in those pre-refrigeration days, I'm not sure but he always accepted it as payment for the beef. I'd like to think it was as much out of kindness to a family short of money but abundant in mouths to feed, as much as any need for or profit to be made from rabbits. The boiling beef would end up in the pot with water and a few handfuls of barley and that was our soup. No vegetables and not much seasoning but a welcome respite, nevertheless, from the usual diet of porridge and oatcakes.

Bella had her own rabbit traps set up on well-known runs. Very simple affairs they were too, with a noose of wire fashioned in such a way that it would loop over the cratur's head and tighten as the beast struggled. Cruel it may sound to some folk, but that's the way it was in the country in those days. Ma would never believe Bella had caught the rabbits in her own traps and would claim they must have belonged to the Rosses at Calhame. She wouldn't have cooked them, anyway. For some reason, Ma didn't make the best use of all the readily available food on our doorsteps and would refuse to skin a hare or rabbit despite the fact we were aye hungry and meat featured very seldom in our diet.

The stone floor of the kitchen was cold to the feet but Ma wove rag rugs from time to time to give a touch of warmth. In the middle of the floor was the table around which four or five chairs lived, accommodating whichever backside got there first. We used the table a lot—to eat, wrestle with the current homework task or play games. Father had his own cushioned chair by the fire—a concession to his place as head of the family. No-one else was allowed to sit on it—except the cat! He was very fond of animals, my father, but didn't hesitate to drown as many kittens as were surplus once the requisite number for keeping down the rodent population was reached. We also had a double-wick paraffin lamp, which, despite its hissing and spluttering every evening, cast its soft, yellow light as a protective mantle over us all. The passing of the days and years was marked by a beautiful, wooden clock—a wedding gift to my parents—and it sat on the mantelpiece between two candles on saucers that waited patiently to be called into service when daylight faded.

In the corner at the back of the kitchen lay the meal kist, a sturdy wooden box that held our essential oatmeal and flour. On a shelf inside it was a brush made out of hens' feathers that Ma used for wiping down any excess flour when she was baking. A rolling pin was also kept there. On the floor beside it, under the half window, was a box with a supply of peats, replenished periodically from the stack at the side of the house. The lower half of the walls were covered in wainscotting and varnished from time to time. The upper half was papered every year by Ma, who liked to brighten the house up with floral patterns in whichever colour she could find.

Behind Father's chair was a press built into the wall where all our foodstuffs were kept as well as assorted dishes and jars of jam. The only other pieces of furniture in the kitchen were a small dresser with doors and drawers, which housed cutlery and crockery and a few cooking utensils, and a washstand and basin. On the big windowsill, at the front of the house, Ma liked to always have a few red geraniums growing in a pot—one of the few adornments in our simple home.

The dresser had an oil-cloth so a daily wipe would do to keep it clean. The back door was usually open and the hens would wander in periodically and hoover up any morsels of food or crumbs of bread. The ashes always had to be emptied, of course, into a pit which Father had long since hollowed out at the side of the house and the wind would whisk them off to fertilize the surrounding fields. The chanties lived under the beds and were used at night when a call of nature summoned the users from their bed. We had a privy of sorts round the back of the byre but, more often than not, we just went behind a distant bush when we needed to. Father would always commune with nature last thing at night before turning in. He would wander off into the dark to some spot or other and look up at the heavens. The vast blackness would soothe him and relieve him of many of his daily worries —and he would take the opportunity to relieve his bladder at the same time!

Most of the children from the village went home at dinnertime but, because we lived so far from school, we were provided with a hot cup of cocoa if we provided the milk. We brought ours in an old-fashioned lemonade bottle, secured with a stopper. More often than not, we were so hungry that our pieces for dinner had long disappeared before school started. After I returned to school following the fever, I had to visit Nurse Michie every day to get my ears syringed and, although this was painful at times, I never really minded as she always gave me something to eat while I was there.

Bella admits to also being ruthless in the pursuit of food. She volunteered to carry old Mrs. MacHattie's water pails into the house for her on her way home from school, not entirely out of concern for the old lady but because of the piece she got at the end of it. She still remembers feeling ashamed, however, at the fulsome praise heaped on her by the old lady's son. Conscience often took a back seat when the belly was empty.

Each child was expected to bring a lump of peat for the school fire and wet clothes and boots were regularly dried over the fireguard following a journey through rain or snow. The same tableau was being re-enacted in most country schools throughout the land during the hungry days of the twenties and thirties when money was scarce but kindness and consideration plentiful.

## Chapter 7

## Simmer Days

As the guns in far off Passchendaele fell silent and men had stopped killing men for a short time, a quiet servant lassie was giving birth to a daughter in the Morayshire Union Poorhouse. In the years that followed, Mary would look at the piece of paper that announced her arrival into this world and wonder what made her different from the rest. The word would scream its malevolence and point its accusing finger at her. ILLEGITIMATE!! No right to be here! Illegal! Unlawful! The stigma would follow her through life and dictate her path. Choices would be removed from her and tongues would wag in her direction.

She wasn't alone. With the absence of reliable methods of birth control, bairns would arrive planned or not, convenient or not, wanted or not to folk married or not. Those born on 'the wrong side of the blanket' were often given their father's name as a middle name, not out of malice but to give the child some comfort that its father was at least known and acknowledged. Some were unnoticeably fused into the existing family, others were passed off as relations other than they were and some were given away to save their mother from 'shame'. The real shame of it was the permanent feeling of disgrace it left on children whose eyelids lowered at each raised eyebrow every time an official form was completed or personal details taken.

Mary was a wee, fragile cratur who trotted along behind her mother and did as she was bid without any fuss. When her mother found a man who would have her, with her shame an all, his one condition was that the child would have to go. A letter was written to acquaintances who farmed at Edinvale to ask if they would take Mary in. 'No strings attached,' it said, and folk who were neither kith nor kin but were open-hearted and generous to an unwanted child, gave her a home. When she arrived, the lady of the house said to her,

"You're tae bide here," and she was handed over.

Mary, then about four, nodded her head and toddled off to hang up her wee coat. And that was that. No formalities. No paperwork. No strings. Just left behind to make the most of it.

"I hope ye'll be a good quine, now!" was the last thing her mother said to her as she turned and walked away.

She never saw her mother again but, whatever her thoughts on it, she would never say. At least, unlike some, she was brought up in a caring family home though, like the rest of the family, she had to work hard to earn her keep. Any extra pair of hands was always useful and, as she grew, she found that there were no shortages of tasks to keep her busy. While the others helped their invalid mother get washed and dressed, Mary would see to the usual domestic chores before setting off for school. By the time she dawdled the three miles, she was aye late and often incurred the punishment of the day. Some teachers looked kindly on her and some didn't, as is the way with folk.

She was a simple quine in that her ambitions were few and her path in life already determined. She knew her place and would seldom be tempted to leave it. For all that though, she was caring and protective towards me and we became friends—each looking out for the other in a world that was often hostile to us both.

If spring was the season of anticipation, summer on the green road was the reward and a grand place to linger. Newly sprung from school, the sweet, intoxicating smell of the whins crackling in the sun filled my head. A thin, red line of old Scots pines stood along the track, defiant against the world. Their gnarled and contorted limbs, rakish and irregular, seemed at once to confront menace from abroad while protecting their own from harm. If the rowan was my mother's favourite tree, then the Scot's pine was Father's, the bark on its branches as knotted and lined as his work-worn hands.

Branchill in summer was a delight, too;—hot, sparkling days, shimmering and simmering, burnishing our faces and limbs the colour of teak, slipping into sultry, dream-rocked nights.

Often the days would be too hot for even playing and we would seek out the shade of our rowan tree, which grew over the burn at the bottom of the garden between the grozart bushes and the peeny roses. It watched us grow from infancy to adulthood that tree and was as much part of home as the house and steading. From its foot we could sit and paddle our feet in the burn and from its branches we could see the world away beyond Branchill. Its fronded leaves spread out across the sky when there was time to lie underneath on a warm, summer evening, throwing up chevroned patterns and silhouettes against the blue. The familiar presence of its ripening berries with their green backcloth, pleased our eye and soothed our childish worries. We knew it kept the witches away and that was a constant relief to bairns growing up in the generation caught between the superstitions of the old and the rationality of the new. Ma's favourite song was The Rowan Tree and it was easy to see why. It *was* sic a bonny tree.

In summer, we had to be on our guard, especially if the day was so hot that nothing much moved. Although they tended to avoid farmland and humans, adders liked to bask in the sun and would often be found coiled on a stony path. We knew enough about them to be very cautious where we trod with our bare feet. You can imagine, therefore, the uproar and panic when Jean burst into the kitchen, scraichin like a banshee and tripping over her breeks.

"Faither, faither, ah've been bitten by an adder. Ma, help me, help me! It's in the privy!"

Her roars could be heard in Forres.

Father shot off his chair and ran out to the yard. He made for the nearest tree and cut a long branch. This he quickly fashioned into a two-pronged fork by cutting a notch from the stem and raced round to the back of the byre.

Meanwhile, Ma comforted Jean as much as she could and tried to get out of her what exactly had happened. Her backside was red certainly and the skin was broken but the poison didn't seem to have travelled far. She minded that her own mother had told her of the custom of dipping an adder bead in water three times to cure bites but she didn't have one nor did she know where to get one.

It could only have been minutes before Father came back. Tears ran down his face and his shoulders were shaking.

"Ah'm nae gyaan tae dee, Faither, am ah?" Jean screamed an octave higher.

Ma jumped to her feet.

"Yir faither's no greetin', he's—laughin'!"

She turned on Father, arms folded and scowling.

"Yir daughter's at death's door an' all ye can do is laugh. Well, I dinna think it's a laughin' matter!"

When Father had got to the privy, he had searched everywhere for the snake but to no avail. The wooden seat holding the bucket had parted company with the frame and left a space under the floor just big enough for one of Ma's hens to take up residence and begin laying. Here she had doubtless felt far enough away from harm to squat in private—until Jean had arrived to do the same. The hen must have been gey annoyed for she had taken her spite out on Jean and pecked her on the dowp before strutting off to find a more suitable place to have her family.

The primroses and wild hyacinth of spring gave way to buttercups and sorrel. We called them sappy soorocks for we used to suck them to drink their sweet juices when we were thirsty. Up on the moors, alpines grew—lady's mantle and mountain sorrel, rock cress and starry saxifrage. Sea coral we cried it and, despite being miles from salt water, thought nothing of its strange name. Meadow pipit and skylark filled the still air with their soaring, joyful trills and even higher, the haunting, mournful call of golden plovers floated across the landscape, bleak and desolate to an outsider but teeming with life to us children who stravaiged it looking for gulls' eggs for Ma or a glimpse of the blue hare.

Summer was also the time for the moors to give up their treasure. Father would take himself off up the road past Rinavey to the peat moss when there were no other more pressing tasks to be attended to on the croft. Over a few days, he would quietly work away, lost in his own thoughts, slicing the peat iron into the soft ground and turning out perfect nuggets of black fuel. One of the jobs I liked best was going up to the moss at dinner-time with Father's piece. He would make a brew of tea in his kettle, so strong it would need a help oot and as black as the peat stains on his hands. We would sit there, father and daughter, drinking in the beauty and peace of the place, both unable to articulate what we felt but sharing an unspoken love for the land and everything on it.

When we were at last released from the constraints of school, one of our first tasks was to climb the road to the peats and laboriously turn and stack each one to ensure the hot summer wind dried them hard before carting them down to the croft to be piled neatly at the side of the house in readiness for the coming winter.

Even yet, on the rare occasions when it is still burned, there is nothing guaranteed more to transport me back to the days of my childhood than the sweet, evocative tang of peatsmoke, stirring memories so precious and fond of family and friends long gone.

Over the Forres road, as well as behind Branchill, the moors stretched for miles and it was here the gentry came to disport themselves in August. As we were stripping off clothes to the bare minimum at the hottest time of the year, they were happit to the chins in tweeds and plus-fours, bonnets and boots.

The moorlands were home to pipits and wheatears, ring ouzels and golden plover but it was the red grouse that drew these men from the south to match their skill with a weapon that could kill a horse against a defenceless bird the size of a hen.

Father would take himself up to the moors with Love bedecked with panniers and, once the beaters had flushed the startled birds from their hiding places and the guns had done their worst, Father would gather up the carcasses and put them into the bags. At the end of a day's shooting, he, like the others, would be given the customary dram as a thank you but, invariably, being unaccustomed to alcohol, would bring it back up, much to the amazement of the gathering. Whisky was regarded then, much as it is now, obligatory on occasions happy or sad and it was the exception rather than the rule to decline it. In the days when lesser mortals doffed their caps to their betters, Father would never have considered refusing an offer of a drink, despite the fact that it made him ill, out of deference to his superiors.

The birds would be dispatched for a second time that day on the overnight train to London to tickle the palates of those genteel lords and ladies who paid dearly for that which we, in our darned clothes and bare feet, could have poached for nothing. Grouse shooting, however, was a vital source of income for most estates then as now and Dallas Estate was no exception. In fact, the bird was so important to the area that it found itself replacing the usual cockerel as weather vane on the roof of the Houldsworth Institute.

Since the fever, I had lost most of my hearing but retained just enough to make out dull background noise and muffled conversation. I don't remember ever feeling aggrieved over my deafness but was acutely aware that I missed a lot of low level sounds, both human and animal, and that was something I simply had to get used to.

When I returned to school after the fever, I was promoted to the middle class where Miss Rhynas reigned. She was kind to me and insisted I sat at the front, the better to hear and observe her lessons. She would allow me to stand beside her when she read the class a story but, being an avid reader by this time, I was always at the bottom of the page before she was and eager for her to turn over.

The walls of the middle class were bedecked with pictures depicting Peggy and John watching tea-pickers in India, dairying in Australia or a Red Indian family at work.

Our day followed the same pattern as most other schools in the north. Morning prayers, Bible lesson and the taking of the register would usher us into each morning. There followed a checking of the previous night's homework with praise or damnation being heaped on the heads of those who had fulfilled their prescribed task—or gone out to play instead.

Tables would be chanted up and down, inside and out, until we were deemed well enough acquainted with them to put them into practice. Then, there followed nearly an hour of arithmetic when our multiplication and division skills would be put under the most intense scrutiny and woe betide anyone who FORGOT—THE—REMAINDER!

Playtime was a wonderful release from confinement for bairns who spent most of their time at home up trees or in burns. Secrets would be shared, food scavenged and loyalties pledged in the too short interval before we had to line up, troop back in and resume our seats. Grammar, composition and infernal comprehension saw us through to dinner-time, which was not given over as much to eating as it was to playing and enjoying ourselves. Our dinners had usually disappeared long before we got to school.

The afternoon session was largely devoted to spelling, handwriting and reading with slabs of history, nature study, geography, art and music slotted in when they could be. The day would be brought to a close with the setting of that night's homework and off we would trot back to our far-flung homes to return the following day to do the same things all over again.

We certainly got a good grounding in the basics of literacy and numeracy and, even yet, on receiving a letter, I can identify the sender as being someone of my own generation, brought up to write in a beautiful, cursive hand and whose spelling would put most younger folks' to shame.

All our books had to be paid for and we were on pain of death to look after them. As soon as we got them home, we would set about scouring the house for a suitable piece of brown paper to cover them. If no brown paper could be found, old copies of the Northern Scot would do.

Art was then, and still is, a mystery to me and I mind spending many's a day trying to draw the second side of a vase to match the first. However careful I was, it never looked right and I must have rubbed the paper into a hole before I finally conceded that I would never make it as an artist.

The cookery room was next door and there we learned the art of baking and cooking simple meals. We would try our hand at plain mince and tatties and oven scones. On the day it was decreed we would make toad in the hole, my first attempt was understandably not terribly successful, with the creation one minute lurching off the plate in a bid for freedom while the next, lying comatose waiting for an unsuspecting victim to taste it. Nevertheless, my long-suffering parents always sampled our efforts with good grace and an encouraging word. By the time their fifth daughter laid her offerings at the family altar, Mother and Father's responses must have been honed to a fine art and their constitutions braced as yet another unidentifiable slorach was laid before them. In truth, I suspect that most of our attempts were fed to the hens.

The middle class, despite my deafness, proved a fertile learning arena, thanks in no small part to the understanding and sympathetic nature of Miss Rhynas. She coaxed and cajoled us through the quicksands of grammar and pitfalls of spelling, refined our infant scribblings into a legible hand and exposed for us the unfathomable mysteries of long division. We learned to sew lap-bags to keep our knitting in and tried to embroider tray cloths with cross-stitch patterns and flowers. We made knickers big enough to house our grandmothers and became adept at threading the elastic through the appropriate channels at waist and leg. My sister Bella had, on several occasions, call to be grateful she had taken extra time and care with hers.

If the weather was conducive and time allowed, we were encouraged to be creative in the school garden. More often than not, this meant some gentle weeding or digging and preparing some new plot for experimental rose or gooseberry bushes. It must have been late summer when Bella found herself gardening monitor, for the grozart bushes were heavy with berries, bloated and filled with juice. She sampled one or two just to check the flavour. Then she had one or two more to confirm her first impressions. The school bell was sounding as she realised she still had two good handfuls uneaten. She could have discarded the evidence but that would have been wasteful. Besides, she had a long road home and was still hungry. With no pockets to come to her aid in concealing her loot, she secreted them under the elastic of her knickers with the dexterity of a practised magician and shuffled her way safely out of school. Forbidden fruit, then as now, always tasted the best.

If you have ever tried to master the art of knitting, you will know the best time to try is not when you are nine and crushed between the elbows of two hefty-armed farmers' daughters. It didn't help to have four pins to control either—three to hold the stitches of the nascent sock and the other one to knit the new row. It was certainly never meant to be done when your hands were sticky with glaur and coated with dust. And, of course, the harder you tried to keep the whole contraption together, the sweatier your hands got anyway and the more the monster fused itself into a damp, impenetrable tangle.

As each stitch escaped from the needle, there would follow a frantic grappling and twisting in a Herculean effort to retrieve it, by which time four more would have made a bolt for freedom, dropping down the rows like a convict going over the prison walls. If that was not bad enough, you then had to negotiate the pitfalls of 'turning the heel' which was usually beyond our capabilities. We either ended up with a woollen sieve or a tube of knitting that went on and on, refusing to turn the corner and was of little practical use except, perhaps, to dress our dolls—if we had any.

Playtimes and dinner times were spent in the field behind the school or over by the Lossie. The boys never played with the girls but we didn't mind. My friends Alice, Winnie, Mary, Eva, Minnie and I were happy if we had a rope to skip over;—

'Two little dickie birds, sitting on the wall,

One named Peter, the other named Paul.

Fly away, Peter, fly away, Paul (exit skippers) (Run behind cawers)

Come back, Peter, come back Paul.' (re-enter and resume skipping ) If you trip on the rope, you're out and have to caw.

When that palled, there was always hide and seek. Whoever was 'het' would shut their eyes whilst the others hid around the playground and field. The leader would then come back, having noted where everyone had stashed themselves and draw with a stick a location map of sorts on the dry ground. It worked well most of the time except when Minnie was 'het' and would always keek. She had found the hiders before the leader had finished her map and the game usually ended in acrimonious debate about who cheated and whose turn it was now. It proved good training, however, for the world of grown-ups when church whists were equally vigorously contested. We had learned not to lie exactly but to tell only as much truth as was necessary.

We sometimes converged at the Lossie where the boys had secured a rope to an overhanging branch. There, they prided themselves in out-jumping each other—or out-swinging or out-falling in the water in spectacular fashion. They, as all boys of pre-adolescent age, pretended not to notice us but always strove to better their last performance whenever the girls came near.

We were so fortunate to have a school positioned as ours was between the peaty waters of the Lossie and the end of the green road, with fields and trees all around and overseeing the village from its vantage point on the hill beside the kirk yard.

# Chapter 8

# Stick Dolls and Burnt Sugar

One of the first things Bella did when she had saved enough money from her wages was to buy a bike. All-steel Raleigh bikes could be had from MacLean's bicycle shop in Forres for £6. 7.6d, or £1 down and then monthly instalments. Some of the income that my sisters were able to earn was sent home in cash or kind to help feed or clothe us younger children and I can't help thinking on the selflessness of Annie and Bella that eased the burden enormously for my parents.

Annie made me a lovely yellow, diamond-patterned jumper when I was about twelve which pleased me so much, not just because it showed off my budding bosom, if I stuck out my chest enough, nor because it was a cheery colour compared to the usual browns, blues and blacks but because she had taken the time and effort to make it. And it was new. And it was mine.

On visits home Annie would bring new-fangled things from Forres at first and then from London when she moved to take up an appointment as cook in a big house. It is a tribute to Ma that all her daughters became excellent housewives and passable cooks, given that she herself had little with which to work and even less enthusiasm.

I had never before tasted these small, round, red fruits that Annie brought home one day and thought them too bitter to be eaten without dunking them first in sugar. It was to be years before I got used to eating tomatoes straight. As cook, Annie volunteered to make jam for her employers. All we bairns, Mother, Father, Auntie Nellie, Uncle John, Willie and Annie Mac and their boys and anyone else who could be press-ganged into service, spent all day picking the sweet red berries which grew in such profusion around Branchill.

Father took the rasps that evening to Forres station when they were put on board the overnight train to Euston where Annie collected them.

Never has jam so fresh been served to lords and ladies in a big house in the middle of a city and never so wholesome and sweet. With all their wealth though, they couldn't have been as happy as we were in our simple croft in the hills.

You had to watch, mind, for weasels lived in the dykes, too. I remember once we were picking rasps at the bottom of the road when Bella grabbed me by the arm.

"Come awa hame, Molly. The weasels are whistling."

She understood enough to know that when they feel threatened, these fearless creatures whistle to alert each other of approaching danger. She told me she'd heard of a mannie that had got too near them and they had gone for his throat. I don't know if that was true or not but it served to make me cautious of them nevertheless.

I had lost at least one layer of skin when I had the fever and, because of that, no body hair ever grew on my legs or under my arms. A few seductive wisps struggled to the surface in the usual places as I reached puberty but for the most part, my skin was as smooth as the proverbial bottom on the proverbial baby and that was a wonderfully convenient state to be in, especially as I watched and waited impatiently for Annie and Bella to finish depilating and deodorising before setting off for a dance. It also meant that some of my nerve-endings were very near the surface.

When it was necessary, our neighbour Willie Mac used to cut our hair—the usual tidy up finished off with a snipping of the short hairs on our necks with his clippers. Every time the scissors touched a particularly sensitive spot, I would slither down the chair, arching my back like a demented cat, till I was almost on the ground. I couldn't then and can't now bear anyone to touch my back at that spot.

Bella would cycle home from Forres on her day off or if she had been summoned home when Ma was finding it hard to cope. She often helped Father with the hoeing and other tasks too heavy for us younger ones. She was probably the closest of us all to my father and in many ways became the son he yearned for.

Having sampled the sophisticated and worldly ways of Forres, she decided I needed a modern look and that Willie Mac's clippers were no longer good enough. She would give me a haircut. She sat me down on the chair, draped a towel over my shoulders and began.

It should be mentioned, perhaps, that what I lacked in hearing I made up for in talking and, without a word of exaggeration, Bella could match my output word for gushing word. We have always been good at talking. Even yet, as soon as we get together, our tongues are at it ten to the dozen with hardly a moment paused to catch breath. That day was no different. There was so much news to be exchanged and gossip to be savoured and embellished upon that the time flew as quickly as her scissors. Rather than leave it to chance, Bella had reckoned she needed something to give my new style some shape. What to choose?

One of Ma's pudding bowls fitted the requirements. There I sat like an ancient druid on his throne with robe and crown. The more we yacked, the more hair fell off and the more I turned my head to hear what Bella was saying, the more she urged me to stop moving about. Of course, each time I turned my head the bowl would slip or alter position and the scissors took off more than they should have. When she had finished, Bella removed the bowl and stared.

"Well, it's yir ain fault. Ye shouldnae hiv fidgeted sae much. Ye kept moving yir heid."

The fringe was fine—the hair was at least out of my eyes. The top was not too bad—short, but not too bad. The sides, however, resembled the remains of a frenzied attack by a tribe of apprentice Apaches, slightly misplaced geographically and not quite perfect in their scalping technique. Every time I had moved so had the bowl and the scissor-happy stylist would snip a bit more off the other side to even it up. By the time she had finished, I had little more than a circlet of hair well above my ears like a monk from some obscure, masochistic order. There was not a lot left to comb.

There is something irreversible about a haircut. There is something decidedly depressing and final about a bad one. I was glad it was the summer holidays.

Father knew when the cows were in season. When they started practising mounting manoeuvres on each other, he took himself up to Calhame to book the services of the Rosses' stud bull. A fine fellow with a coat of sleek, black hair, he had a high conceit of himself that suggested he expected to be treated with respect. He usually was. He counted among his clientele most of the females in the neighbourhood and performed his duty in a desultory fashion and with, some might say, consummate ease. There was usually no need for anything other than the most minimal of courtship preliminaries and the whole performance would take no more than a few seconds. As entertainment went it was better than nothing and I could just about observe the proceedings if I climbed the stairs, moved the bedroom chair to the centre of the room, put three books on top and stood on them on my tiptoes to peer unsteadily through the skylight.

On the mantelpiece in the kitchen Ma always kept a note of when the cows were served or when they were due to come into season. In time, of course, curiosity demanded an answer.

"Fit does 'served' mean, Ma?" I ventured.

In the time it took me to articulate the question, the skelp was already flying through the air and landing round the lugs. I and the others eventually learned to avoid the subject even if we had little idea of why Ma got so agitated. Her reaction, of course only fuelled our curiosity.

Reproduction, two-legged or four, was never discussed, alluded to or hinted at in the home. All around was evidence of the renewal of life amongst the animals and any pertinent facts or salacious tit-bits were gleaned piecemeal in the playground from some loon who had access to his older brother's vocabulary and worldly knowledge. Some of the lassies would chip in with their pieces of information but never, of course, in front of the boys and over time enough of a picture would emerge as to who did what to whom, how and what happened afterwards. Despite that, it was not unknown for a quine from up the country to give birth without having the faintest notion of how the child had got there in the first place. I grew up believing you could have a baby every day if you wanted to until I was put right by Bella.

Once a week, more often if money could be spared, I would run into the village with one of my sisters to relieve Menzies of some of their supplies and replenish our larder. It was the kind of shop that had everything. Bread, candles, paraffin, tobacco, pencils, sugar, salt, loose tea—in the days before it was parcelled up in wee bags—and glasses for lamps could all be purchased at Menzies. Sunlit soap, Cleansil for washing blankets and broken biscuits were stocked. Needles, yarn, envelopes and scrubbing brushes were all available.

Our cousin, Lewis Skene, helped in the shop and was only too happy to supply Annie and Bella with a supply of broken biscuits any time they felt hungry on their way home. It was grand having an obliging cousin and they reckoned they were on to a good thing. And indeed they were.

Father didn't see it in quite the same way, however, when he received a considerable bill some weeks later. Neither girl could sit down for the regulation fortnight when he discovered what they'd done.

There was always something to see along the green road if you knew where to look. Curiosity had to be slaked and the inquisitiveness of bairns satisfied. If there weren't new calves to be wondered at, John Ross would have his array of heifers for us to christen with imaginary names that took our fancy though I doubt he ever had the time to know or care what we called them.

Often he would have his pigs in the field and one particular day, Bella and I took it into our heads to jump the burn, climb the fence and take a closer look at the piglets lolling, as piglets do, in the mud. We were not to know that their father was in the field with them. Nor were we to know that, for some reason known only to himself, he would resent the presence of two strangers and see us as a threat to his progeny. He took one short, inquisitive look and gave chase.

Bella knew that once a boar got hold of you, he wouldn't let go, locking his sharp teeth into your leg, or arm—or worse— in a grip so tight that the only release from it was the loss of a considerable lump of your flesh. The two of us took to our heels, neither looking back at the boar or each other but making for the gate at the end of the field.

Why it didn't occur to us to vault the fence to safety I don't know. It probably had something to do with the terror fuelling our stampede and the panic, not only in our breasties, but in our bowels, bellies and every other bit of our bodies, which prevented rational reflection and lucid thought. A bystander may have been impressed by the speed of our flight and the agility of our trampolining over the gate at the bottom of the field as the boar bore down on us with gathering speed. After a brief rest and a checking that all our limbs were intact, the same bystander may have been astonished at the range of gesticulations and grimaces two small girls had in their repertoire. We thumbed our noses at the boar, which had by this time skidded to a halt at the gate, thwarted and perplexed. We stuck out our tongues, flapped our fingers from our temples like demented sparrows and whistled and ya—ha—ha—ha—ha'd at the pig, more out of relief at our narrow escape than malice for the beast.

As we sauntered home, we congratulated ourselves on outwitting the creature though I don't mind us ever going into his field again.

When Ma went on one of her monthly sorties to the Guild, Father would take himself off to bed for forty winks. 'A flap' he would cry it and Meg and I would set about raiding the press for some jam sugar. It came in coloured, crystallised lumps and was guaranteed to appeal to both the eyes and palates of bairns who rarely had money for sweets. The trick was to achieve a balance between satisfying our craving and not incurring Ma's wrath by depleting her stocks so much that she would notice. You could eat these lumps in many ways.

There was the straightforward 'crunch hard and swallow quick' method when you first started and your greed was at its height. As your taste buds accustomed themselves to the sweetness, a more refined way was the 'rolling round the tongue and teeth' technique, a sure way of maximising damage and decay but so delicious nonetheless. If you were beginning to suffer sugar overdose, then the more leisurely 'holding it under your tongue till it melts' was the system you would use, holding your breath in anticipation of that bursting of the reservoir of concentrated syrup which lasted only a few seconds before you were forced to swallow it but had to be repeated, again and again, so delightful was the taste.

In the winter, we would heat the poker in the embers of the dying fire and dip it into a poke of sugar. Then we would spend many happy minutes picking out fragments of burnt sugar from the bag and feeding them into our waiting mouths, which drooled with anticipation, like a dog looking longingly into a butcher's shop.

Skirlie was another favourite. A pan would be placed carefully on the fire and some fat melted. Into it, Meg and I would tip some oatmeal and mix it up. In the absence of anything else, it would fill our ever-hungry bellies for another five minutes. Father never clyped on us tae Ma and we loved him for it. We all loved him anyway.

The fire in the kitchen was always on as it was our only means of cooking and source of heat. The lum was never swept in the conventional sense, and looking back on it, it was a miracle it never went on fire. When Ma reckoned it needed cleaned, she would light some old pages from the Forres News and send them up the chimney to set the soot alight and clean it that way. We were lucky. Had there been a major blaze, we would have been hard pushed to put it out and, as we were at least six miles from any form of fire appliance, could easily have lost our home and quite probably our lives.

Most of the time, we didn't have a toothbrush and, as a result, our teeth were ignored. Ma had already lost her own and wore fausers. Father's teeth had, one by one, deserted his mouth and those that were left were stained with nicotine and blackened with decay.

When a toothbrush was purchased, we all shared it and, if money didn't stretch to toothpaste as well, we would dip the brush in soot from the lum and rub furiously up and down and side to side, skirping our clothes and walls with black specks in the process. Gradually, our teacher would extol the virtues of oral hygiene and urge us to invest in Gibb's dentifrice, which came in a flat round tin and burst into a lather of pink bubbles when mixed with water. By the time we got round to using it with any form of regularity, irreversible damage had already been done to our teeth but we continued anyway as it was not an unpleasant taste lingering in your mouth on the way to school.

Once a week, Ma would take one of the chairs from the kitchen, turn it upside down and lean it against the leg of the table. Then the two-handed wooden tub would be brought from the barn where it lived for the rest of the week and would be placed at an angle into the cross-pieces of the upturned chair. Into that would go hot water from the kettle and our weekly wash would be done using a wooden wash-board. 'Stubborn stains,' of which there would be many, were attacked and dissolved by vigorous rubbing with knuckles and a bar of red Sunlit soap. Once the 'wash cycle' was done, the water was changed and the rinsing began. Excess water was pressed out when the clothes were, one by one, fed through the jaws of the mangle. They were then strung up on a rope or fence to let the elements do the drying.

Most of our clothes didn't need ironed but, on the occasion that Annie or Bella had a petticoat or blouse inherited usually from others who had outgrown them, the box iron would be brought out.

As the name implies, it was a flat contraption with a box at the end in which iron slugs found a home. There was always a pair of those so that, when one was in use, the other would be in the fire being heated up. The end of the iron had a hinged lid and, by inserting a poker into the hole at the end of the slug, it could easily be lifted in and out without burning the user. Being metal, each retained enough heat to iron a garment or two before being exchanged with the other and this tedious process of heating and reheating continued until all the ironing was finished.

Bella was, on one occasion, grateful that she had taken the time to iron her underwear. Being Bella and always having something else to do, she had been in a particular hurry to get to school one day. When she arrived, breathless and hot from running, she quickly opened the buttons of her coat to hang it on the peg—and just as quickly closed them again. In her haste to get to school, she had forgotten to put on her pinafore.

Now, I don't want you to think that we always went to school in pinafores and gym slips or the like. I've no evidence but suspect Bella must have fallen heir to someone else's cast-offs, someone who had had the good fortune to go to the Academy in Forres and merit a uniform. At any rate, whoever it had belonged to originally was irrelevant now as it wasn't where it should have been. For the rest of that hot, never-ending day, my sister sweated and stewed and had to suffer the discomfort and impracticality of wearing her outdoor clothes indoors. Geography and gym were performed with difficulty and playtimes were spent in unaccustomed isolation. She resisted every attempt by the teacher to divest her of the coat until she was safely back at home where she could, at last, uncover her embarrassment.

Whites, or the nearest we had to whites, were draped over the whin bushes for the sun to bleach and, when we went to bed on top of our newly laundered sheet, the sweet smell of the warm outdoors would drift around the room and soothe us to sleep.

In the summer, when it looked like the weather was set fine for a few days, the blankets would be stripped off the beds. The large iron pot, which for most of the year lurked in some dark recess of the barn, providing refuge for hens and cats, was ceremoniously brought out, dusted down and filled with water from the burn. Then it was placed carefully on the fire we had all helped to make. Into the wooden tub, with its brew of Cleansil and peaty water, went each blanket in turn. Ma, or more usually Annie, Bella, Jean, Meg or I would roll up our skirts and climb in and begin trampling.

No worker could have felt more content. We were all together for a few, precious hours, our feet warm and clean, blankets de-flea'd and revived, leg muscles exercised and toned, lungs filled with coconut-scented air and hair teased with the warm, Moray breeze. If you had offered me a wad of money then, I would not have taken it in exchange for a day like that—nor would I now.

In turn, each blanket was washed, put through the mangle, rinsed, fed into the rollers again and finally hung over a rope in the field. A hot, dry day had to be chosen because the blankets had to be put back on the beds that night. We had enough blankets for the three beds and no more. Bedding consisted of a bottom sheet with a blanket on top, which made coorying under the covers gey rough on our faces. The blankets frequently wore into holes and stayed that way until someone got round to darning them.

In the winter, a blanket was never enough to keep out the cold from the permanent winds that whistled constantly through the gaps beneath the doors and down the chimney. Our coats, which normally hung on a nail behind the bedroom door, were used as a second layer of warmth on the beds. And Father's redundant jackets and any other old clothing were frequently stuffed up the chimney to act as a makeshift draught excluder.

Cold feet in bed often prevented sleep but could be thawed by the presence of our version of a hot water bottle. A surplus lemonade bottle would be gradually warmed up on the binkies at the side of the fire. Water would then be heated up in the kettle and poured into the container into which a stopper would be driven. The receptacle was then fed into one of Father's socks to protect our feet from burning and up the stairs we would trot, oblivious to any knowledge that our homespun methods were not practised the world over.

Because mattresses were stuffed with the chaff left over when the threshing mill had done its business and pillows were filled with feathers, we were rarely alone in bed. Fleas had a comfortable home and a ready supply of food. Our vests and liberty bodices often bore the bloodied remains of those who did not survive our continual, nocturnal scratchings and rubbings.

Sleeping in close proximity to my sisters and always being within head-touching distance of my class-mates, lice were also always tenants in our hair. The weekly Sunday night delousing followed the same pattern, year in, year out. Paraffin not needed for the lamp was applied to each head in turn. Brown paper was spread on the table and, with the thorough raking of the comb loosening the inebriated beasties, we vied with each other to count the most as bodies dropped on to the paper. The whole process had to be repeated every week as re-infection was inevitable.

Home remedies were always employed to counter common ailments and the nurse, and less commonly the doctor, would only be summoned if it was thought we were in acute danger.

With an abundant availability of vitamin-packed fruit like rasps, blackcurrants and hips, we were, for the most part, pretty well immune from colds and the like. If we did fall prey to the occasional sore throat or belly-ache, Ma would make up a hot blackcurrant drink and pack us off to bed. If the throat was really sore, one of Father's unwashed sweaty socks was turned inside out and applied to the appropriate place. It was reckoned to have curative properties—either that or it acted as a placebo comforter to the sick child who would have recovered anyway but always felt better after a spot of attention.

Frequently on winter mornings, Ma would have to apply cotton wool dipped in warm water to our rheumy eyes which would have their lashes stuck together with 'crows' meat' from the cold during the night. Eyes, and any matter which exuded from them, were called 'crows' meat', I suppose because crows would often peck at the eyes of new lambs. At least our sticky eyes could be gradually cleaned and brought back to full working order with a little time and care.

We had no toys save those which my older sisters managed to buy from their meagre earnings. For the most part, my doll was a stick enshawled in a scrap of material surplus to the requirement for which it was bought. Imagination is a wonderful play-mate and that doll and I played happily for many months until I eventually tired of her diffidence and lack of enthusiasm and cast her aside, with no remorse whatsoever, to climb a tree or have a shottie on Bella's bike or annoy my brother.

A favourite game Meg and I played was stotting a ball, when we had one, against the outside wall of the house.

'Plainie, clappie, roll the reel, the backie, right hand, left hand, touch your heel, touch your toe, birl around and through you go.'

We derived enormous pleasure from just having a ball, a wall and each other.

Imagination, resourcefulness and adaptation were the keys to us never being bored.

Hogweed, decapitated and cleaned, was a very effective pea or barley or stone shooter. Iron bands from unused and long-forgotten barrels were prised off, uncoiled and fastened with rope to the high-lacing boots we wore in the winter-time and made satisfactory skis. Our turns were rarely parallel nor our style recognisable or approved by the vividly-clad aficionados who haunt the ski slopes today but we had fun and the satisfaction which comes from hitting on an idea, putting it into practice and revelling in the fact that it works.

When all else had been exhausted, there was aye a spot of climbing to be enjoyed.

The roof of the byre was at just the right angle to be shinnied up with my child-sized fingers and thumbs just the right size to grip the underneath of each row of slates in turn till the summit of the roof was conquered. From there it was a straightforward manoeuvre to stand up and scamper along the tightrope that was the ridge. Annie Mac from the neighbouring croft would invariably come running out, wiping her hands on her peenie, flailing her arms about like a wayward windmill to encourage me down but, unable to hear her entreaties, I would cheerfully return her waves, as much impressed by her friendliness as I was oblivious to the danger I was in.

The roof on the fald over the binder shed was made of corrugated iron and heated up nicely in the summer. It was pitched at just the right angle to make a slide—if you first climbed the aforementioned byre roof and braced yourself for the drop. The landing from it, however, had to be negotiated carefully, for if you went too far to the left or right, your bottom would land on the remains of the old pig-sty and suffer considerable lacerations as a result. Meg rarely would agree to accompany me on any assaults on the roof and so soloing up the pitch became my speciality while reading continued to be hers.

As she was nearest in age to me, we played at houses as my sisters had done, using broken bits of crockery, which, when they had served as cottage or castle, would be ground down even further for grit for the hens.

## Chapter 9

## The Pig in the Sidecar

Ma, despite having at least as comprehensive an education as my father, preferred the light-weight thrills and revelations from the pages of The Womens' Weekly, The Weekly News and The People's Friend which she got, second hand, from the wife of the gamekeeper at Dallas Estate. These kept her, to some extent, in touch with the outside world—or at least with one perspective on it. Father, on the other hand, liked his newspaper, The Northern Scot, The Forres News or that window on the wider world, The Press and Journal. These he would scan, savour and digest and use the information he had acquired to converse with any local or stranger that happened by.

One such regular caller, if an annual visit could be called regular, was the Princess Mary man. We called him that because he was always talking about the Royal Family and the young princess in particular. Where he came from and where he went when he left us, we never knew. His name was James Austin and I would call him a gentleman of the road. A gentleman he certainly was for he was always polite to even us children and kept himself largely to himself. He was well-spoken and well-educated and Father enjoyed talking to him and sharing his enlightened views on the world. He did his own sewing and mending and all he asked of us was a bed in the straw out in the barn and a bowl of porridge to send him on his way in the morning.

I mind on anither mannie, too, who appeared from time to time. He would turn up at the school—a fragment of humanity damaged beyond help by gas and shells. Religion must have been his saviour, for he would accompany us home along the green roadie—the Ettles, the Rosses and ourselves—none of us scared or worried that he would harm us, and he would aye say,

"Now cheeldren, we'll just seeng heems all the way home."

And, without question, we did.

There were many beggars and tramps who happened by from time to time and Ma and Father would always show kindness to them. Travelling tinkers would set up their bow tents at the foot of the Wangie. Stewarts and MacPhees they were and they would go round all the farms selling clothes-pegs and bunches of heather and mending tins and the like. They were extra hands to help with harvesting and tattie-lifting and their bairns would join us in school for as long as their fathers had work in the area. They were accepted for who they were—'stragglers from Culloden' some folk said—and we welcomed them into our midst without fuss.

A lot of information could be gleaned from our local papers. Whether it was the fanfare heralding the occasion at Darnaway Castle of the Summer Fete and Bazaar or the appearance of Madame B. Goldrick and her Exhibition of Fashions. Stranded skunk wraps sold for £5.15/- and Hudson Bay red foxes for £3-19-6d. I'm not sure if the skunks in question had been left high and dry in some exotic land and, when rescued, threw themselves at the mercy of their saviours and didn't mind too much relinquishing their coats for the benefit of genteel ladies in Morayshire. I suspect they were just striped in appearance. Red foxes were plentiful in the Highlands and I wouldn't have thought we would have had to import them all the way from Canada to dangle, forlorn and lifeless, over the shoulders of matronly ladies in our part of the world. As for the goings-on in Darnaway, we were as likely to go to the moon as have time and money to cavort around for a whole afternoon when there was work to be done at home and, at the time of Madame's appearance, I was lying unconscious in Forres hospital anyway, where the fate of her skunks and foxes were of little importance to me or my family.

If I had to be in hospital at all, then I suppose 1927 was as good a time as any. The horse-drawn ambulance had recently been replaced, by public fund-raising and the generosity of the Red Cross, by a new motorised vehicle. Central heating, electric lights and x-ray equipment had been introduced to Leanchoil and gifts of flowers, cakes, rhubarb, vegetables, rabbits, pillows and fruit were being regularly donated and acknowledged by the matron.

Luckily for me, coinciding with my release from hospital, the National Institute for the Deaf was galvanising itself into an active body and launching an appeal to raise £25,000. Underwriting this was their pledge 'to secure a national envisagement of the whole problem' and to 'mitigate its (deafness) effects to the individual.'

Had I had the inclination or vocabulary to read further, I may have heaved an enormous sigh of relief that, should I ever need to lose weight, which, in itself, was highly unlikely, then I need look no further than the following catchy advertisement:

<u>'How I Rubbed Away a Stone of Fat from my Hips and Abdomen in Two Weeks' Time.'</u>

'Thanks to a lady friend who had studied herbisterie, I learned the secret of a harmless plan which enabled me to rub away with ease, a stone of useless fat in only weeks. One draw of quassia chips and 3 ounces of cirola bark extract; boil, strain and stand. Rub in a circular motion. I soon grew too slender for my clothes and had to have them taken in. Each time you can almost see some fat melt away.'

Had I been conscious at the time, this would have been a great comfort to me. As it was, I had no useless fat to lose and what I did have was falling off me without any help from an apothecary.

Father borrowed a bicycle if he needed to go any distance or visit one of his brood in hospital. But on the day he decided that our menagerie would benefit from the addition of a pig, it didn't take much smeddum to jalouse that that particular mode of travel was of little value in the transporting of the pig home. As far as we knew, pigs could not ride on a crossbar nor balance on the carrier at the back, though I confess I don't remember anyone trying it out. Young animals could be bought for up to 22/- at Hamilton's Auction Mart in Forres in those days and Father planned to fatten it up for selling later.

Willie Mac, his wife Annie and their sons were now our neighbours at Wester Branchill. Kinder folk you couldn't meet. They had moved in when the Camerons had left. Willie was a valued chiel in many ways—he helped us with the harvest, as neighbours did then, and he was the proud owner of a motor-bike—with a sidecar!

On the Tuesday in question, Willie and Father set off on the contraption and made good time on the road into town. Once at the mart, livestock was examined and compared with other livestock, old friendships were reacquainted and yarns exchanged. Drams were forced down throats and more and more drink insisted on and reciprocated as the day wore on. Father never took drink that I can mind, not out of any religious conviction but simply because we couldn't afford it.

As the market day began to wear on and, one by one, the cronies appeared more ancient, more trusty and certainly more drouthy. They had sat boosing at mony a Forres nappy and, though I can't say for certain, Willie was, if not foo, certainly not empty. I can only surmise as to how happy he was, unco or otherwise. The two made to set off home, Father sober because he was and Willie consciously sober as only an inebriate can be. They boarded the motor-bike with Father and the newly purchased pig in the side-car.

As they passed Leys Cottage on the road home, Auntie Annie observed the spectacle from her window. She was later heard to remark that it was just as well the evening was quiet for thon motoring machine was taking the width of the road. All went well until the final bend on the final brae before the turning into Robbie's road, when the intense concentration needed to steer the bike began to waver. Trying to keep the bike from going over into the ditch, caution gave way to misjudgement and, while the bike took the corner perfectly, the wheels of the side-car hit the bank and toppled over.

Pigs are, by nature, highly-strung and excitable creatures. The one Father had bought was showing every indication of being in need of sedation even before he got him into the side-car. It had squealed and squirmed since it left Forres and, after a terrifying journey over pot holes and ruts, travelling at speeds no pig should have to travel at, it was little wonder that this piglet was hysterical by the time the driver rounded the bend and lost control.

Sizing up the situation, it thought it would save its own bacon and made a lunge for the open hill. But Father, paying no heed to his own safety, manfully held fast to the pig's trotter and, despite its writhings and wrigglings, managed to hold on till Willie had righted himself and his machine. As to the smell of drink and the state of his clothes, not to mention the mental turmoil of the animal, one can only guess at his explanations to Ma. I would like to think that she accepted his story without question, but I hae ma doots!

Father, like most of his kind, was an early riser. He would get out of bed at 5.30. every morning from spring till autumn and an hour later during winter. Ma would see to his breakfast. It was always the same—oatmeal brose or porridge with a cup or two of sweet tea and bread, or more usually, oatcakes, and jam. There was aye plenty jam. By the time we bairns got up two hours later, he would have the cows fed and watered and Love the mare given her bruised oats and a drink from the burn. Ma milked the cows before we went to school and one of us did the evening milking when we came home.

His main meal of the day was between eleven and twelve. Tattie soup made with milk, followed by neeps, more tatties and sometimes a boiled egg and oatcakes. There was always plenty tea as the kettle was boiling away all day long.

When we bairns came home from school, we would all have supper together. If there were more bottoms than chairs, the youngest would stand and we would sup our porridge, each eager to exchange the day's news and be happy to be back together again. The tin basin would be lifted on to the table, filled with hot water from the kettle and the dishes would be washed, dried and put back into the press before we were allowed to scatter and follow our own ploys. The pots would find a home outside the back door until they were called into service again.

Beside the dresser stood the wash-stand. It had a back and sides and harboured an enamel basin and red Sunlit soap which every morning we were press-ganged into using. Ma would line us up and inspect our necks and pity help the ones who had missed a bit. Jean must have given her neck just a quick dicht for Ma caught hold of her and sent her back to have another go.

"Aye," says Bella, "it's as black's the Devil!"

The room went quiet and the look on Ma's face sent Bella running for cover. She knew she had said the wrong thing. No mention of Auld Nick or his following was ever tolerated in our house, just in case the mere suggestion of his name was enough to invite him and his hellish legions into our Godly home. When she thought the stooshie would have died down, Bella tip-toed back into the kitchen to retrieve her school bag.

Ma was waiting for her.

"Jist ye wait 'til yir faither hears fit ye've been saying."

Her voice was beyond anger.

When Bella returned from school that afternoon, Father was waiting for her and gave her such a tongue-lashing—the one and only time he ever fell out with Bella, who was inconsolable not because of the row but because she had disappointed her beloved father whom she worshipped and who, in turn, loved her probably more than the rest of us because she was always there at his side, ready to do his bidding and work as hard as any son for him.

Ma was the one in our house who dished out punishment if it was deemed necessary. The only time I ever mind Father taking his hand to me was the day I broke the glass on the paraffin lamp. I would have been around eight at the time and hungry as usual. Father had been sitting quietly reading his paper and I had tried to squeeze in behind his chair to peruse and perhaps plunder the press. The bread and jam was kept there and was usually the only thing available to keep us going 'til the next meal. Not taking enough care when opening the door, the edge caught the table and knocked over the lamp. Whether it was the fright he got as the glass smashed on the stone floor or the money, scarce at the best of times, that he knew he would have to find to replace it I don't know but he jumped to his feet and lunged at me.

At first I stood my ground, then made to run round the table, followed in hot pursuit by Father. I must have got a fright, too, because, as I ran, the tell-tail trail of terror began trickling down my leg and the faster I ran, the faster I dribbled. He caught me and pulled down my wet breeks and gave me the one and only leathering I can remember him giving me.

Once the work of the day was done and the homework finished, Ma would make us a drink of Fry's cocoa. I still have the bread knife I bought with the coupons from Fry's cocoa these many, long years ago. Up the stairs we would go with our candles in their saucers to kneel at our bed-side. There followed a rushed incantation of the Lord's Prayer before clambering into bed. If Jean and Meg were still at home, we would be two at the head and one at the foot of the bed and it wouldn't be long before determination to eavesdrop into adult conversation deserted us and we fell asleep.

Inside his plated long-johns and semmit, which Ma always warmed for him in front of the fire, Father was shielded against the biting wind that often whipped at his kindly face and the ravages of the elements that made him old before his time. A grey, collar-less shirt covered his back and heavy breeks were suspended over his shooders with working men's galluses. Tackety boots with steel toe-caps enveloped his home-spun stockings. A flat cap protected his thinning, curly hair from sun and shower and, with his pipe in his pocket, my father would be out there in all weathers, working and coaxing his 27 acres of land until it could yield no more. He was shorter in stature than Ma and had not an ounce of surplus fat on him, which was not surprising given the amount of hard, physical work he had to do.

I often wonder what he thought of, my father, as he walked up and down the field behind his plough. Was he content with his life or did he ever feel cheated out of the chance of education, which would have changed his life in so many ways? Did he feel resentful at all us bairns depending on him for food and shelter and keeping him on the endless treadmill of farming?

I don't remember him ever being anything but cheery and kind to us all so, if he had any black thoughts, he never showed them. He always worked hard and long and never faltered if there was a task to be done, either for ourselves or for our neighbours.

He would on occasion climb, purpose-like, up the hill behind Branchill. Finding a rock to sit on, he lit his pipe and took a long puff. He looked around him. Below, on his right, the gentle hills rolled away to the blue while, to the left, the land sloped down beyond Forres to the North Sea. The voices of his bairns drifted up from the homestead below—happy, laughing voices that brought a smile of contentment to his weathered face.

Behind him, he felt the spirit of generations of his people—hard working folk kyauvin' awa at the land, their backs near breaking with the toil. As he looked away into the distance to a time not yet come, he couldn't know that future lives with his blood in them would bear the name Robbie in his honour. Some of his children and their children and theirs, would work with their hands, fine-boned and artistic like his, to create fine things. Others would inherit from him sharp mind and resolute determination and achieve recognition in their chosen field—law, medicine, science, engineering and education. All would owe a great debt to, and hold in much affection, this gentle man of the soil.

At his funeral, it was said that Robbie had never been heard to utter a bad word against anybody and I'm sure that was true.

He was loved by his neighbours as much as by ourselvelves.

## Chapter 10

## The Seventh Day

Although not regular attenders at church, Mother and Father observed the well-established ritual of keeping work to a minimum on Sundays. The beasts and ourselves would be fed but all other work that wasn't essential could wait till Monday. The water would have been drawn from the well the night before. The kitchen table would be scrubbed and Bella and I would wait till everyone had gone to bed before sweeping out the kitchen floor and scrubbing it till it shone. Sunday was a day of rest and if anyone needed a rest from the relentless toil it was my father.

We bairns, if the weather was good enough, walked to Sunday School at the United Free Church, which stood at the foot of the Wangie, surveying the flood plain of the Lossie and the village beyond. The other church, St Michael's, was the Church of Scotland and most of the village went there. On the east bank of the Lossie, just opposite the kirkyard, there was a lovely waterfall running down from the rocks above and folk used to call it St. Michael's Well. The water was pure and reputed to have special healing properties, though I canna mind it ever being put to the test.

The congregation was sparse and strewn about the kirk, with families refusing to sit anywhere other than their traditional family pews which generations of their kinsfolk had occupied since memories could mind. This made the minister's job more difficult as sermons had to be delivered at quarters close and far and his head would swing from left to right to make sure all his charges got the benefit of his message, sometimes skewering a sinner with a stare that would curdle cream.

The Sunday School, comprising sometimes only half a dozen of us, would retire to the back of the church before the service started to be addressed personally and to receive some appropriate homily or other urging us to choose the straight and narrow. The choir, of which I was a member, then swept to the front of the kirk and took up our places beside the organ. Starting from cold each time, the organist pedalling furiously would have to heave and sweat to get the beast to cough into life and, with much spluttering and wheezing, the first hymn would be intoned. In spring, we ploughed the fields and scattered; in summer, paid homage to all things bright and beautiful; autumn, of course was largely given over to harvest thanksgiving while in winter we carolled at the top of our voices—often discordant, often lisping but never less than enthusiastic.

Some of the local loons, leaning more to the secular, would entertain themselves by trying out the bikes left outside the church. Safe in the knowledge that they had a whole hour to amuse themselves without being disturbed, they raced and chased each other on our prized cycles—and, on one occasion, on Bella's.

Before she had left to go back to work, Bella had made me promise not to use her bike nor let anyone else have a shot. But I must have sorely needed redemption that day because off I went with the bike to Sunday School and left it with the others, safely round the back of the manse. When I returned, it was to find a very sorry looking Grant Stuart looking at an even sorrier-looking buckled, broken bicycle. He had taken the machine for a wee shottie and being something of a novice, had mis-judged the turn in the road. Apparently, the somersault had been spectacular, with Grant flying through the air over the handlebars and over the fence. He landed tapsalteerie in amongst the corn with a dent to his pride but otherwise unhurt.

Bella's bike, however, did not come off so well. The front wheel was badly buckled and the shining chrome considerably scratched and cratered. Grant had the good grace to persuade his father to replace the wheel and he did his best to polish up the bits that were bashed but that bike was never the same again. It was sometime later that Bella discovered the main frame had snapped and that her pride and joy was not safe to ride. I don't remember her being angry with me and I don't remember getting into trouble for taking the bike without asking but I do remember the awful feeling of guilt and that I had abused the trust she had in me and caused her so much trouble and upset.

My dear sister Bella, I'm so sorry about the bike.

After dinner on Sundays, if it was fine, we would persuade Ma to take us on a picnic. Loch of the Romach was only a mile from Branchill but it seemed to belong to another world. The steep hillsides came right down to the water and one or two trees dipped their branches into its peaty depths. In earlier times, it had been the main site for illicit distilling in these parts and, even yet, I like to imagine it still has more secrets to give up than those we already knew. With us we took a kettle, the accoutrements for making tea and a scone or two, oatcakes and, if Ma had been to the village, a bit of cake. The best part of our picnics was that we were all together. We climbed anything that could be climbed, paddled with our skirts up above our knees and lit a fire to boil our kettle on. Even Ma, who was usually too busy for fun, joined in, laughing and sharing our joy with us.

Ma always wore her long hair up in a bun held in place with kirbigrips or pins. Though her hair got greyer the style stayed the same. I don't remember her ever getting it cut but I suppose she must have done from time to time. Her work-a-day tweed skirt came down to her ankles and concealed woollen stockings that were attached to her steys by suspenders. She wore bloomers and a vest and hand-knitted jumpers like the rest of us. On the few instances she went out, she wore her good skirt and blouse under her long, black coat, which did for church, guild meetings and the occasional wedding. She always wore a hat, as most women did in these days, and flat black shoes on her feet.

Poor Ma, I never really got to know who she was. She was our mother who dished out kindness and clouts in equal measure but never gave away much about what she was thinking and, by the time I was old enough to think about her as a person, I had left home and was trying to make my own way in the world. I wanted to ask her so many things about herself but, as so often happens, I left it too late.

Father would seldom accompany us—I don't know why for certain but I suppose he relished an afternoon to himself free from the constant drone of female tongues. He also suffered badly from migraines and would thole the pain stoically until beads of sweat ran down his ashen face and he had to run to the back door to retch. He probably took every opportunity he could to get some rest. He would shave on a Sunday, carefully scraping his cut-throat over his jaws and under his chin. No matter how much time he took over the procedure, he would always succeed in missing a bit—the same tuft behind his ears—every week.

Sometimes, Meg, Jean, Sandy and I would put on our Sunday best, which in truth was not that different from our usual clothing, and go for a walk to the well below Big Branchill. On one such occasion, a loon who worked on the farm would be sitting on the hillside, smoking a pipe.

"Oh look at Beel Black learning tae be a faither," I would shout.

We all laughed, none more than Bill himself, who couldn't have been more than sixteen at the time and, no doubt, had an inkling that there were better ways of practising parenthood.

Other Sundays would see us traipsing up the road past Auntie Nellie's and Uncle John's to the peat moss. It was so peaceful to just lie on the heather and listen to the birds. We would come back armed with sea coral which I loved arranging and re-arranging in my imaginary houses and Ma was always finding bits of it under beds and behind chairs.

Our neighbours at Calhame were the Rosses and they were exceptionally kind to us. There was a big family of them but that didn't stop Mrs. Ross always having room for one more at the table or time for a visit. They also had a gramaphone. That might not seem terribly special nowadays but then, when we had no electricity never mind entertainment, it was nothing short of a miracle to find music and song coming out of a funnel. There was a selection of 78's, too, with bands and singers popular at the time. Mary Ross, one of the daughters in the family, would lift me up to look down the speaker.

"Can ye see the mannie in the music box?"

Nod, nod, went I, not sure if I could see him or not but anxious to please her for the trouble she was going to on my behalf. The rotating dog of indeterminate pedigree, listening patiently for the voice of his master, wasn't much help. He just kept peering into the horn as perplexed as I was.

At least two of the Ross sons lived in a loft above the nearby stable and they were avid smokers. We called it the berrick, I suppose a corruption of 'barrack.' They would allow me to invade their home to collect all the cigarette cards from the mountain of empty packets littering the hearth. These were numbered and in sets and I greatly enjoyed shuffling, sorting and resorting them. There were pictures of varieties of cattle, birds and various animals with, on the reverse, information about them. These added to my general knowledge and, I suppose, instilled in me the pleasure that could be gained from having a hobby and the anticipation that would crescendo as each time I strove to find that elusive card that would complete the set.

Father's one vice, if that's what you would call it, was his pipe. He smoked Black Twist, a strong, evil-smelling substance that came on a rope, from which he would cut a length and grind it between his work-hardened fingers to a consistency suitable for the pipe. He would light it with a spunk and settle back to enjoy his smoke. You always knew when Robbie was having a break from his work. Wisps of blue smoke would spiral up from behind a dyke or a bush, giving away his whereabouts. He would allow himself an ounce a week and once that was finished, he would resort to smoking tea, pilfered from the caddy on the mantelpiece, which produced a reek even more noxious.

Bella would bring him tobacco every time she came home from Forres for a visit. He would stand leaning against the jamb of the door waiting for her and she, in turn, would indulge his love of a joke by hiding.

"Well, well, Izey, there's no need for ye tae hide. Onywye, I could hear yon tongue clacking since it left Forres!"

Father had a mischievous sense of humour, always ready to make a joke and have some fun. He would ask Bella, "Heard any bars lately?" and the two would revel in the latest jokes doing the rounds in town, though, truth to tell, Bella probably didn't understand the bawdier ones—at least I don't think she did. We were all green at that age when it came to innuendo and suggestive comment. Ma would sit knitting in her chair, quietly tutting at the more explicit stories but harbouring her own sense of humour and probably sharing the tale with Father when we had gone to bed.

Ma kept hens—about twenty—who, in theory lived in the hen house but in practice had the run of the place, inside and out. White Wyandottes, Rhode Island Reds and one bantam, which she had given to me to look after. One day, I came home from school and couldn't find my pet anywhere. Ma looked unusually crestfallen and led me to the back door where my charge was dangling by the feet—very quiet, very still and very dead.

Ma was apologetic and explained that she had shut the door on it without realising it was behind her. Its neck had been broken so there was nothing that could be done. We grew up amidst life and death—hens and ducks necks were wrung regularly and unwanted, superfluous kittens were unceremoniously hit over the head or drowned in the burn without a qualm.

The hens and ducks were released every morning from the hen house. Most of the time I knew where their eggs were but when they were clockin', Ma would gather about a dozen eggs and swap with a neighbour to vary and improve the strain. Ma knew by the change in the sound a hen made that she was broody and ready to sit on her eggs. She would take her into the cart shed and shut her into a coop, eliminating the light with a sack across the door. She would feed her corn, sprinkle water on the eggs and turn them and there the hen would sit for three weeks. She wouldn't mess her nest but would oblige by performing her toilet outside.

The ducks liked to lay furth of the hen house and I would gently put my small fingers inside them to check if there was an egg with a shell already formed. Then I would watch where they went. They always seemed to know when they were being watched, those ducks, for they would devise many and varied places to lay to confuse me. I would eventually track them down to a nest over at Annie Mac's where they must have thought they would be safe from thieving hands. No such luck, for Ma took their eggs just the same. She would gather the eggs and use them for baking. I only remember the occasional duckling making it to hatching but I'm sure there must have been enough to continue the succession.

Before the eggs went under the hen to be incubated, Ma would hold a threaded needle over each one in turn and, if the needle swung back and forward, it would indicate a male chick. If the needle went round, it would be female. Ma only wanted female eggs so natural selection was interfered with to ensure a brood of future egg-layers. We rarely had eggs to eat. Father would get one every day, though, and the minister, when he descended on us. Some would be used for baking and, on the few occasions there were surplus, they were sold for cash or exchanged for goods in the village shop.

We usually had two cows. If they were not with calf, they would be milked twice a day—by Ma in the morning and one of us at night. Sometimes we had to tie the tails to their hind legs to prevent a skelp on the face. The milking stool kept in the byre would be placed by the cow's flank and the two front teats would be milked, followed by the two back ones. Once it looked like that was all the milk she was going to give me, I would wet my index finger and thumb and carefully pull them down either side of the udder to strip all the milk out. Cows were fickle craturs, holding back or letting down their milk depending on whether they liked your technique or not—or whether they liked *you* or not. If the calf was a female, it would be sold as two milking cows were sufficient for our needs. The stirks were kept and fattened up over a few years and then sold at the mart to provide goods which had previously been luxuries but, in our rapidly changing world, were fast becoming essentials.

I knew when the cow needed the bull, for the signs were there to see.

"Peggy's running," I would tell Ma when the cow tried to ride on her companion's back and father would make the necessary arrangements to have her seen to by the bull. When the calves were born, they would be allowed to suckle from their mother for a short while and then be weaned. I would drop my hand into a pail of milk and scoop some into the calf's mouth, each time lowering my hand towards the pail until, eventually, the calf learned to drink from the pail itself. We couldn't afford not to have a plentiful supply of milk, for it had so many uses and was one of our staple foods.

Some of it would be taken into the milk house just inside the back porch and strained through a fine sieve, to filter out hairs and dirt. It was then poured into a plotted basin—scalded and sterilized with boiling water. Some then would be put into small bowls with rennet added to separate the curds and whey, the latter used for baking and the former mixed with cream to make junket and spread over oatcakes. The rest of the milk was put into two basins for use on porridge or for drinking.

Sometimes, but not often, Ma would make butter. She would pour milk into the wooden churn which had paddles attached to its sides. The handle was then turned slowly and at a regular pace, with the turner looking from time to time to check the consistency. A little salt would be added then the butter removed and put on a flat, wooden slab from where it would be separated into 1lb. lumps. Ma would then decorate the top with patterns from her butter pats and wrap each one in greaseproof paper to be sold or exchanged for food in the shop. For some reason, one of the things she bought in exchange for her butter was margarine—a very poor substitute for the real thing. Maggie-Ann we cried it and that was what we used most of the time on our pieces.

I only mind Ma once making cheese. Instead of adding salt, she would add rennet to the churned milk. When it was turned enough for it to start solidifying, a mould was lined with cheese-cloth and the mixture poured into it. The cloth was covered over and the parcel taken out to the cheese press, which lived, then and now, at the side of the dyke at the end of the house. The iron handle on the press was turned slowly, gradually squeezing out the whey. It was tightened daily until all the moisture had been removed. She must have sold that, too, for I canna ever mind us eating our ain cheese.

Every year, Ma would take it on herself to paper the kitchen. The passage and their own bedroom was papered, too, but not as often. Any floral pattern or colour would do, depending on what was available in MacKenzie and Cruickshank in Forres and how much money could be spared. Our bedrooms upstairs under the coom ceilings had plaster on the walls and that was white-washed from time to time. They were sparsely furnished. Both had holes in the walls where the fireplaces had once been but these were never used in my memory, not even on the coldest nights. As well as a cast iron bed, with its chaff mattress and feather pillows, there would be a chair and a chantie under the bed. On the mantelpiece, a candle on a saucer offered the only source of light and a nail on the back of the door sufficed as a wardrobe. It was enough. We didn't have many clothes and those we did have were either on our backs, on the washing line or ready for the rag-bag. A few books would lie in a pile in a corner and these I would delve into when boredom got the better of me. I mind one favourite was 'The Way of an Eagle' and I would read that book from cover to cover until I knew the story as well as the author.

At the top of the stairs, under the skylight, were a few odds and ends—cardboard boxes and a suitcase or two—waiting patiently to be called into service. For the life of me, I don't mind them ever being used, those cases, but someone, sometime must have had a need for them.

Lizzie and Bella Masson, bonnie quines

Bella Masson and Robbie Skene on their wedding day

Bella's Bike (l. to r. Sandy, Molly, Jean, Meg and Bella)

Father and Love

Ma and hens----and Father's best side

Robbie with Sandy at Branchill

Molly aged 10

The threshing mill

Robbie Skene – 'he was loved as much by our neighbours as ourselves'

The Skenes off to a wedding (Back row – Bella, Jean, Annie; middle row – Molly, Father, Ma, Meg; front row – Sandy)

Loch of the Romach

Molly

Johnny

Panto Band at Bleicherode – Johnny far right with mandolin

Preparing the sports pitch outside the compound at Bleicherode

Molly in Ostend 1945

Railway Pier, Oban 1948

Ma with Auntie Nellie and Uncle John

Auntie Nellie with Molly

The late Mary Chalmers, Elgin

Molly with Molly Douglas, Elgin

Oban Badminton Club 1949

Bella and Molly – still yacking and still bonnie quines

# Chapter 11

# An Education of Sorts

As August drew to a close, there came the awful dawning, as happens to every child the length and breadth of the land, that carefree days were coming to an end. It would happen slowly with a casual comment here and an incidental observation there. Then, one day, you would be gripped by a feeling deep in your bowels that wouldn't go away. After breakfast you would be shoe-horned into clothes that were neither comfortable nor practical for tree climbing or roof-traversing and you would know that today was the first day back at school. With each year that passed, another of my sisters would graduate to the world of work, leaving me to walk the green road alone. Sandy was still too young to go to school and he and I would only have two or three years together, before I, too, departed for Forres.

As in every school, there are some children for whom the daily rituals of arithmetic and grammar are incomprehensible; children whose brains take longer to process information or who simply don't possess the necessary tools to know where to start. These 'slow learners' were treated very sympathetically by Miss Rhynas, who gave of her time and adapted each lesson to their needs, long before the practice was accepted as the norm. Her successor, however, made little effort to continue her work, preferring to give these bairns manual tasks such as keeping the fire topped up with peat and helping clean up around the school to keep them out of the way and save himself the effort of trying to teach them.

The new headmaster came to Dallas School when I was eight. I will not honour him by giving his name but those of us left who suffered at his hand will know his identity. It will be branded on their souls, much like the victims of any other tyrant.

By this time, I had long accepted my deafness and had found strategies for coping with school. I was allowed to sit as close to the teacher as possible and she would always make a point of facing me when explaining some point or other so that I could read her lips and gauge her expression. I not only managed to keep up with the rest but succeeded in winning class prizes with unfailing regularity. From my first day in the qualifying class, however, the new dominie seemed to take a dislike to me and would find any excuse to lift the lid of his high desk.

Lochgelly, as far as I'm aware, is a harmless sort of place. The kind of place you might want to visit or even retire to. But, for me and generations of my kind, the name engendered fear of the most palpable kind—hot sweats, cold sweats, tremor of limbs and wetting of knickers. The name was stamped on the 'preferred method' of chastisement in schools and its use was not only condoned but actively encouraged by all in authority. The belt was two feet of tough leather with thongs on the end, deliberately positioned to snake round the wrist and fingers on the moment of impact. It was used as routinely as his references to the Bible by the new master.

When Jessie, a quine of the same age as myself, couldn't pronounce 'determined', he thought he would make an example of her. He hauled her to the front of the class and, looming over her, demanded the correct response.

"De—ter—mined," he instructed.

"De—ter—minded," quivered Jessie, becoming more and more distressed.

"De—ter—mined," he shouted.

"De—ter—minded", Jessie repeated, by now rigid with fear.

"Read it, girl! De—ter—mined, de—ter—mined, DE-TER-MINED!"

Jessie's tongue just couldn't articulate the right pronunciation.

The longer the stalemate went on, the redder his face got and the louder his voice; the longer the stalemate went on, the more poor Jessie was confused and kept repeating herself. The battle went on for some considerable time until the ringing of the bell announced it was dinner-time and Jessie and the rest of us trooped outside, thankfully rescued from further confrontation.

While he strove to explain an algebra problem or point of grammar, he would stand with his back to the class and, relying on lip-reading as I did to follow lessons, I found it impossible to understand what he was saying. To keep up with the rest and being eager to learn, I was forced to ask my neighbour what had been said. That was enough to incur the wrath of my 'educator' who, more often than not, pulled me out of my seat, ridiculed me for not hearing, piled two boxes of library books on top of each other to get better purchase and then strapped me across my small, ten-year-old hands. I didn't know then and, for the life of me, still don't know why he did it.

Good teachers have an affinity with their pupils and try to see the world through their eyes. Our master had no such feelings for his pupils, only a streak of sadistic evil that would surface periodically. Even on a good day, he obviously disliked us.

Was it because he had been subjected to harsh discipline himself as a boy?

Was it because he had been wrenched from the comparative genteel suburbs of Edinburgh to mould bairns of country folk, most of whom spoke in a tongue foreign to him? Was it because, at only twenty-six, he had found himself in a job that he detested and realised he would be doing for the rest of his life? I can't say. All I know is he hated me with a vengeance and never missed an opportunity to humiliate and punish me. He would resort to sarcasm before giving a child the opportunity to explain. As we lived so far from the village, we were given cocoa at dinnertime if we had provided the milk. As happened from time to time, we would have none.

"Please sir, our cows are dry," I would inform him.

"Well give them a drink, then," he would answer, smirking at my discomfort and pleased with himself for making a joke at my expense.

George was in our class and the master called him 'the goat' to his face and to ours.

"Stand up, goat!" he would bellow and poor George, feet shuffling uncomfortably on the wooden floor, would rise and hang his head with embarrassment. A muckle loon, George was at that awkward stage when he was neither boy nor man. His clothes would always look too small for him—jacket buttons straining to hold him in and trousers failing to conceal the feet end of his spindly shanks. His voice was one minute himself and the next, his father. Tufts of fine down were beginning to randomly sprout on his face, which, at the slightest hint of attention, would glow like the fires of hell we were always being threatened with. The master would throw chalk at him if he didn't get a satisfactory reply to a question or goad him with the blackboard pointer. On more than one occasion that I can mind, he chased the loon round his desk till one or the other was exhausted.

The day had started like any other. The usual registration and Bible story preceded the singing of hymns and chanting of tables. The week's spelling words were delivered with practised concentration and the tortures of handwriting suffered until it was of an acceptable standard. I had always found geometry easy and was engrossed in my work and oblivious, initially, to the commotion fermenting behind me. The hypotenuse and its attendant relationships had got the better of George and no amount of wheedling, sarcasm, threats or temper could enlighten him. The master's face was flushed and twitching as never before. White froth was gathering at the corners of his mouth and his eyes bulged. He dragged the poor loon out to the front of the class and shook him by the shoulders in a frenzied rage. His control finally snapped and he flung George to the corner of the room. His head smashed off the heavy, full-sized blackboard, resting on its castors. It, in turn, ricocheted off the corner of the wall and split from top to bottom. George sat dazed for a second or two then lifted himself off the floor. The dominie, by this time trembling and ashen-faced, was full of apologies and tried to help the boy to his feet. George brushed himself down, walked calmly to his seat, collected his possessions and walked out of the room.

He never came back to school again.

The untold damage to a child in his formative years at the hands of a sadistic brute cannot be measured. In those days, dominies were held in the same high regard as ministers, lawyers and doctors and were never questioned or challenged as to their behaviour or treatment of us. As a consequence, we rarely reported such ill-treatment to our parents for fear of getting another clout at home. This particular bully continued to teach, if that is the right word, for many more years in a school in the next county to ours. I hope his pupils there fared better under his care than we ever did. Despite him, I won the dux prize in my last year at Dallas School. Scott's Ivanhoe, it was—a book I have never been able to open without remembering these days of perpetual terror and unmitigated cruelty.

Work always stepped up a gear during the late summer at Branchill.

If the weather had been fine, Willie Mac would bring his gelding over and yoke him alongside Love, our mare. The binder needed two horses to pull it and we would do the same for him. A Bisset, it was, made by the Blairgowrie firm who supplied most of the farms in the north-east.

Father would scythe up one side of the field using his hand scythe to provide a straight edge for the binder to work against. Then the binder would be turned on and followed the line, cutting the corn, now the colour of faded gold, as it went. A horizontal windmill, fixed on to the binder, with six or seven paddles, would scoop the corn on to the moving canvas sheets and they would start carrying the sheaves up to where they were tied with twine and shoot them off the top of the rollers. Two sharp knives cut the twine at just the right moment—and would have done the same to Jean if Uncle John hadn't noticed her disappearing under the canvas strapping. When the machine's rollers were turned off to allow the horses to turn at the top of the field, we would be given a ride on the binder, sitting on the wooden bench, which was at just the right height off the ground to enable us to drum our heels on the coarse, corn stubble. It was so painful it was almost pleasurable and we kept coming back for more.

Jean, however, couldn't have been paying attention to the fact that the machine had been switched on again, for back she toppled on to the canvas and it was only the speedy reaction of Uncle John sitting on the high seat, that saved her being parcelled, bound and gagged—for good! Father had to dismantle the whole contraption to get her out and, as I wasn't around at the time, I would only be guessing if I said he patted her on the head and told her to go off and play somewhere safer.

Living with farm implements obviously carried inherent dangers and I often think we were very lucky to survive our childhood with fingers, toes and other bits intact. Mind you, when I thought it would be interesting to see what happened when I removed the pin holding the grubber in place, I didn't foresee that it would release a spring-loaded bar which clouted me under the chin with such force that it permanently altered my jaw, leaving me with a profile not out of place on MacBeth's 'blasted heath' and making me an authentic star-turn at Hallowe'en.

(My chin has always been a source of amusement in the family but it has had its uses, too. All my grandchildren, and great grandchildren, have cut their teeth on it, as it is just the right angle, size and thickness for a good chew!)

Once the stooks were bound and tossed on to the ground, the women folk and we bairns would stack them in fours, with the heads pointing up the way. We all worked together at the harvest, Father, Ma, our neighbours and bairns, to gather our precious crop before the weather broke.

They would be left like that to dry out for a week or so then father would assemble a big frame over the cart and he and usually Bella would go off to the field with Bella forking the stooks up into the cart while Father laid them out in precise formation, working his way into the centre and stacking them three high. The cart was then taken to the yard at the back of the barn where the stooks were arranged, ears inward, into a dome shaped haystack. We usually had four or five of them, tied with twisted rope and weighed down with stones.

The highlight of the autumn, as far as I was concerned, was the day the travelling mill came to Branchill. It was certainly an important day for my parents but it took on the air of a carnival for us youngsters. We would all be running about, getting in everybody's way. I would scoop up Puzzie MacKenzie from across the road, in mid-run. He was only about two at the time and I was very fond of him. I would carry him around with me all day—him hanging on to my neck and me trying to see where I was going over the top of his tousled hair.

It was not necessary for every farmer to have his own threshing mill unless he had many fields put down to corn. Even then, he would only have the need of it for a short time every year. The travelling mill covered all the small crofts and farms in the area and it meant that neighbour helped neighbour with his harvest, getting the job done quickly and with a great deal of fun, banter and camaraderie.

The day would start early.

The mannie would arrive from Craigmill with the monstrous machine, bigger by far than anything we had on the croft. It had a muckle great wheel which, using a series of cogs, drove a belt which, in turn, powered the rollers. Father would have got in a supply of coal to power the brute and then, when the steam was up, it would splutter into life, shaking and juddering for all it was worth. Rats, who had made their homes under the stacks, would run for cover and our cats would be out having the time of their lives hunting them down. Two loons would cut the twine on the sheaves and feed them on to the rollers, which would, in turn, vibrate as they moved the sheaves along. By slicing, riddling, shaking and winnowing, the ears of corn would be stripped from the stalks and bagged by Father and Nath Stuart, Jock Masson, and Willie Mac. The straw that was left was separated into strae for animal bedding and feed and the chaff, which was left after the husks were removed, was used to fill the family's mattresses. It made a comfy bed when it was stuffed into ticking and covered by a sheet.

All the men folk in the area, related or no, would gather on threshing day and though not paid in money, would be well fed by Ma and the other womenfolk.

Ma would buy big mealie buns from Forres and these would be offered to the workers with lashings of butter and jam at mid-morning. They would all be given a fine dinner of soup, meat and tatties with yet more tea and buns in the afternoon. This feast would be repeated when the mill did the rounds of all the nearby crofts, — Wester Branchill, Rinavey, Big Branchill and Coldhome. It was an enjoyable and sociable time, with men, women and bairns all mingling and mucking in and the work made easier by the good-natured banter and teasing that always seemed to fly between neighbours.

The strae stack was kept near the mill-gyang, which had been used by folk long ago when they had milled their own flour using horses and waterpower. There was no water in it now.

Once the corn was bagged, most of it would be taken to Craigmill to be ground into flour and oatmeal. The remainder was lifted into the loft to be stored for the winter, when it was crushed in the fanners to provide bruised oats for our mare. Every time I thought I was being helpful by trying to carry a bag on my back, it would topple and spill as I attempted to heave it up to the loft. What I lacked in inches though, I made up for in determination but Father eventually took the sack off me. I was already very roon-shoodered from straining to hear. I suppose he didn't want to make me worse.

Each year would bring its own problems and unpredictability. The year I was nine, the summer was glorious. Rainfall during early June was light and July's weather was ideal for ripening grain and contented beasts. However, just as Father was gearing himself up for an early harvest, the rains started and largely spoiled the crop. The bad weather continued through September, hampering the hay making and generally setting everything back. We just had to make the best of whatever the weather threw at us, some years good, some bad, some disastrous.

Once the corn was safely in, we still had neeps and tatties to lift. That was a back-breaking job, if ever there was one. The neeps would be thrown into the back of the cart with Bella and my father working together, one leading the horse, one lifting the turnips. The youngsters would help pass them to be topped and tailed with the snedder, a small scythe which Father used, before feeding them into the neep cutter to reduce them to a better size for the cattle. For some reason, I thought the handle made a good swing—until the day the blade came down on my finger and cut it to the bone. The tops of the neeps were ploughed back into the ground and the year's crop was taken round the back of the byre to be stored for the winter in the neep shed. Nothing was wasted.

The tatties were the same. Once all the shaws were cut, they were raked to the side and burned to prevent the spread of blight or other diseases. The potatoes themselves were lifted into the cart and taken round the back of the steading to be stored in the tattie pit. They were then covered with straw and finally turf to keep them safe from frost and out of the light, where they could be kept all winter and used as necessary.

We got a week off school every October to help with the tattie-lifting, such was the importance of them as a mainstay of our diet. Folk could still mind the terrible days of the potato famines in the last century and how it reduced many communities to starvation, forced migration or death.

The green road in autumn was no longer green. Its mud, baked hard and the colour of cinnamon, was cracked and lined like the faces of the old folk. The once vital pools along its length were now still, weed-strewn and covered with oil that had leached from the surrounding fields and hovered on the surface like the mist on the hills. The roddens stippled their blood-red across the landscape, which was gradually transforming its mantle of green to a counterpane of orange, yellow and gold. The bell heather on the moors carpeted the ground with purple and stretched further than you could see to places beyond your ken. Its wiry stems tore at your legs if you chanced to walk through it and its bonny flooers tore at your hert.

The peewits no longer performed their acrobatics overhead and the summer swallows had begun to melt away southward to warmer climes. But the redwings were there, and the fieldfares roaming the moors and banqueting on blaeberries the size of bools. The red grouse which had evaded death in August joined forces with pheasant and partridge to add a further splash of colour to the moors while bracken and bramble painted russet and black across the hills.

That green roadie became my companion and confidant through my growing years—years that were taking me to adulthood all too quickly, and I knew its every mood and secret, just as it knew mine. It led me away from home and family but always brought me safely back.

# Chapter 12

# Spreading Wings

I canna mind the first time that I went to Forres for certain. We visited Auntie Annie, of course, but without transport of any kind getting to the town depended on the occasional bus that was beginning to travel the road or the offer of a lift from a neighbour. All my sisters had started their working lives helping Auntie Annie and Ma would often arrive for a stay when things got too much for her at home. Bella must have only been left the school a few months when the doctors decided that my poor hearing might improve if my tonsils and adenoids were removed.

I stayed at Leys Cottage the night and Bella and I set off for Inverness on the bus in the morning. It was a great adventure for me travelling so far from home and seeing a different world. It was also fine to be with Bella, just the two of us, for a day or two without anyone else interrupting our blethers. In all truth, I can't mind much about being in the hospital but when I was recovering the sister in charge took me to the bottom of the ward and showed me the sink.

"Turn the tap on, Molly, and if you rub your hands thegither, you can make the water warm."

I stood transfixed as water trickled out, cold at first but gradually getting warmer. I stood for an age rubbing away for all I was worth, letting the warm liquid run over my hands. I had never imagined that such a thing was possible, only being used to washing in cold water straight from the burn. I marvelled, not for the first time, at the miracles of progress that were beginning to creep into our lives.

The other thing that stayed in my memory was the sweet taste of the ice-cream the nurses kept insisting I swallowed. With my throat still raw from the operation, it was the only thing I could have—not that I objected. Ice cream was an unknown luxury in our house so I made sure I got as much as I could before going back to auld claes an' porridge.

On the way home, I stayed the night again at Auntie Annie's. When I awoke, I was so ashamed to discover my mouth had bled all over the pillow and did my best to wash it off. I knew it would probably fall on Bella to do the laundry but, when I think on it now, I more than likely made the stain worse. She worked hard, Bella, in the butcher's shop with Uncle Alex and in the house for Auntie Annie, and on her day off, in the fields with Father.

Forres has always lived in the shadow of Elgin a bittie, but I loved going there. It was close enough to Branchill to be familiar but far enough away to be an adventure. We never had money to spend, of course, but just looking in the windows of shops was enough. The town stood on a fertile plain with the gentle Rafford braes behind and a mile or so from the mouth of the great river Findhorn. Varis had been known and written about as far back as the map-maker, Ptolemy, from the land of the Pharoahs and the forests and moors surrounding it were favoured for hunting by the old Scottish kings. King Duncan had his camp there.

Elgin became the choice, however, for monasteries and churches and many of the gentry preferred it for their country homes. So it developed and grew to become the largest town in Moray, with its cathedral, castle and arcaded buildings erected by prosperous merchants, while Forres remained largely a market town.

Forres had always been highly thought of as a shopping centre, though. Even folk living as far away as Sutherland bought their goods from merchants in the town in days before there were any shops in their own county. Weekly markets were held every Tuesday and acted as a convivial meeting place for fermers and crofters, glad of the chance to get into town for a whilie to meet up with others and to peruse the beasts on offer. The town had boasted gas lighting and a public water supply since the middle of the last century and all news and forthcoming events could be read about in the 'Squeak,' as we cried the Forres Gazette. In the years when I was growing up, thirty passenger trains a day arrived and departed from Forres as it was a junction for the lines from Inverness, Keith and Perth. Many's a time snow would block the line over Dava Moor and the train couldn't get through.

A cholera hospital had been built on the Waterford Road but fortunately had never been called into use. Instead, it had been turned into a training laundry and dressing and knitting school where girls attended to learn domestic skills. Manufacturing grew, with firms like Taylor's providing the local folk with tweeds and tartans, blankets and bedcovers, according to necessity. The sizeable North of Scotland Chemical Works made sulphuric acid for agriculture and gave employment to many folk who had been forced off the land to look for work. There was a Bobbin Mill, too, supplying reels for the jute industry, which was beginning to expand further south. The Waterford Flour Mills did on a grand scale what our travelling mill did on a small and ground and bagged flour ready for use to whoever needed it and had the money to pay. In the century before I was born, Forres already boasted a steam sawmill, a gas works, a slaughterhouse and barley and oatmeal mills. A hydropathic had been built on Cluny Hill and served yet as a useful landmark to take your bearings from.

There was the Tolbooth, of course, and in front of it, the Market Cross that most towns of any size had in these days. The one in Forres was copied from the monument to Walter Scott in Edinburgh and had been finished around the middle of the 1840's. The year I took the fever, the first picture house opened in the town.

The Academy stood behind the High Street and educated all those in town and country who had passed their qualifying exam. At least, all those who could be spared to continue their education and whose folk had enough money to pay for it. Of our family, Annie, Bella and I all passed but not one of us got the opportunity to take our learning any further. We didn't expect it and held no resentment against those who did. Any children from Dallas who went to the Academy had to cycle there and back every day in all weathers. A regular bus service was beginning to meet the needs of the community but didn't fit in with school times.

When Annie left school, I was still a toddler and can't mind much of her comings and goings. She found work first at Hillockhead then at Grangehall and obviously liked the place enough to stay for many years. When Bella left to go to Forres, she stayed with Auntie Annie for several years, leaving to make room for Meg when it was her turn, and finding employment instead at Darnaway Castle.

The castle is set in woods on the far side of Forres from us and there, Bella learned much more than the domestic skills she was employed to use. The lads who worked as grooms and gardeners would always be game for a joke or two and catching out a green scullery maid was usually high on their list.

It must have been Bella's day off—which often wouldn't begin 'til three in the afternoon—because it was quite dark when she got back. The shadows fell across the courtyard, making it difficult to see clearly. She was quietly making her way across the yard when something moving in the corner caught her eye. A ghostly spectre was hovering under an upstairs window and flapping its arms in alarming fashion. An unearthly howl was coming from its throat.

She had heard the story of the castle's ghost often enough. An earl, who had lived many centuries before, had lost his first wife and had remarried. He already had a son but when a second was born to his new wife, she realised that her child wouldn't inherit the lands and titles of Moray. She did, as others in a similar position had done in these days, killed the heir and since then, the spirit of the unfortunate lad had taken to haunting the courtyard. It manifested itself at regular intervals and many swore they had seen it.

"If ye think ah'm scared of ye," proclaimed Bella, "ye must think ah wis born yesterday. Onywye, fit kind of ghost needs a bicycle tae stand on or uses the sheet that ah mended yesterday?"

And with that, she went to her room. After a few minutes she thought she could hear scuffling outside her door. She looked around to see if anything had been moved or tampered with but found nothing. She got into her night-clothes and was just about to put out the light when she thought she saw something moving under the blankets. Carefully pulling back the covers, she disturbed a very big and very ugly frog that obviously hadn't got there under its own steam. She decided not to scream, which of course the scufflers were waiting for, but lifted the brute, opened the door and flung it out into the passage. Of course, the loons were all crouched round the door and got such a fright it was they who screamed and yelled, waking the housekeeper and, no doubt, half the household.

The following morning, nothing was said but Bella quietly and contentedly got on with her tasks while her tormentors went about theirs, suitably reprimanded and subdued. They wondered what they could do next to rattle this new maid. The answer was very little, for, although new to the place, Bella had more common sense than some folk twice her age and an uncanny knack of being able to put back in their place those who had dared step out of it.

A hedgehog had been rescued from an untimely death in one of the many snares about the place and had been given a box to itself in the kitchen beside the Raeburn. It had been baptised Henry Rupert, the same name as the current earl and, of course this had allowed much ribaldry and coarse comments that would otherwise have been frowned upon. Days of hard work were broken up by fun and capers amongst those 'downstairs' and it was undoubtedly that which kept them all going.

Domestic service was a hard initiation into the world of work, but when our time came, my sisters and I rose to the challenges and made the best of it. We had to.

There was nothing else.

# Chapter 13

# The Turning of the Year

When snow was on the ground, lying deep and cold, we had to make our way to school by the main road—longer to walk than the green road, but at least free from drifts to fall into or hidden holes to wrench ankles. On such mornings, a strange creature could often be seen slinking out of the door and taking off along the road. Meg and I, two years apart in age, had one scarf between us and no hat to keep out the bitter wind that, Father claimed, blew straight from the North Pole. Each end of the scarf opened out just wide enough, if you stretched it a bit, to fit a child's head. So with Meg's head in one end and mine in the other, the two of us would set off, bobbing and bowing, tugging and straining, each trying to keep in step with the other like novice ballroom dancers practising their manoeuvres.

Christmas in these days was not as big an event as New Year. Decorations were few and those that we had were hand-made. My sisters, brother and I would become hunter-gatherers for the day, disappearing over to the Loch of the Romach where we knew holly trees grew and coming back, each armed with enough to decorate the fireplace and the two or three pictures we had hanging around the place. We didn't have a tree but religiously hung our well-darned stockings, full of optimism, from the mantelpiece. We knew instinctively not to ask for much and our usual presents were an orange, penny and a wee toy. As each sister left home, she would sometimes bring home something bigger.

No lassie could have been happier than I was when Annie brought me a right bonny pink dress with flowers and short-puffed sleeves, just in time for the Christmas party.

When Sandy was about four, I came home to find my sisters had returned for a few days. Sandy was playing with a new barrow.

"Far did Sandy get that?" I wanted to know.

"Oh," said my father, "Santa brocht it."

"Far did he see Santa?"

"Over behind the calvies' fald," replied Father.

Off I raced but, despite looking high and low and all places in between, couldn't find any trace of him. I didn't mind Sandy having something and me not, though, as I'm sure Sandy would have shared the barrow with me.

If he hadn't, I would have borrowed it for a shottie when he wasn't looking.

Still anxious to see Santa, I crept down in the night. Father had his answer ready. His blue eyes danced with mischief.

"Noo, if ye hid only got here half an oor ago, ye wid hae seen him for sure."

A cousin of Ma's had a shop over Archiestown way and would send a parcel of presents, including sweeties, to us every Christmas. I don't even mind her name now and I'm sure she's no longer around to read this. If she were, I would thank her from my heart for what she gave us. It may have been a small gesture to a distant relative but her kindness made Christmas a magical, special time for us bairns. It also removed from my parents any worry they had at not being able to give us anything. They probably didn't realise that the gifts they had given us couldn't be bought anyway and, unlike our toys and trinkets, lasted us a lifetime.

Each Ne'er Day, Father would go off with Willie Mac to the moors to shoot a blue hare. It was something he always did, probably a tradition passed down over many generations and so deeply ingrained he had long stopped even thinking about it. Back he would come eager to show us his kill but we never had the pleasure of sharing it with him. Ma would point blank refuse to skin and cook it. He never showed his disappointment in Ma—never in front of us anyway, but he must have felt aggrieved after the bother he had gone to.

Work didn't stop on the croft when the growing season was over. Fences had to be repaired, the drains and ditches cleared of weeds and mud, the beasts still had to be fed and cared for and all the implements used throughout the year had to be mended, sharpened or checked over. If the ground wasn't hard with frost, Father would take the chance of turning over the soil to plough back the stubble from the harvest and any leftover turnip tops that were still lying around. There was always a trail of gulls following the plough, their raucous cries piercing the still air and their dark-hooded heads triggering a memory of tales told round firesides long since. Folk living at the foot of Cairngorm believed that the black-headed gull carried the souls of the good and, as their sins faded as they neared heaven, so too did the blackness of the gull's head until, by winter, it was a pale brown.

One thing we looked forward to in the winter was sitting round the fire with Ma and Father. The dark would have settled by four o'clock and, once supper was over, we would have long evenings with little to do. The peats glowed red in the gloom and our old lamp gave out just enough light for Ma to knit socks by and us to see the expressions on Father's face as he told his yarns. And good yarns they were, too. He would tell us of his own boyhood, bringing us closer to the grandparents we never knew.

His family had moved to Rafford when he had left home and it was there they remained until work and worry wore them down and the kirkyard claimed them. Rafford was actually nearer to Branchill than Dallas was but didn't have a school or shop so we tended only to pass through it on our way to Forres or to visit cousins. Father would tell us of the old days and tales his own father had told him as a loon. Days when the ordinary folk lived in houses without floors, ceilings or chimneys, when the windows were made of very small, fired panes of glass if you were lucky to have any and the only blinds on them were a piece of linen threaded on a string. They burned peats to keep warm on a fire in the middle of the room and, as often as not, also used fir blocks as fuel. To brighten their homes, they would hold split pieces of fir over the fire and fasten them on to the walls to cast a soft light.

As the years passed, they learned to make candle moulds into which they would pour tallow, which was the fat from slaughtered beasts, and that sufficed until paraffin lamps made them redundant. Many of the womenfolk would be employed in making plaidin, the coorse cloth that most country folk wore.

"I mind on the days——," he would begin, and off he would go on another story.

"I mind on the days when horses warnae fed on oats and sic like. The women wid cut all the whins doon an' feed them into a holie in a quern stone that wis jyned on tae a lang shaft. The shaft wis yokit tae the horse which, poor thing, hid tae walk roon an' roon until the stone hid ground the whins doon. Aye horses hid tae mak their ain supper in yon days!" and we would all laugh.

"I mind ma faither telling me that when his faither wis a loon, ferm servants were paid £2 for a year's wark an' servant quines £1. The lads wid get their meals cairried tae them in the fields three times a day, in a' weathers an' wi' nae clocks tae watch their lives passing, they rose wi' the cockerel an' went tae bed wi' the hens. They hid nae oors tae guide them but could tell the time by watchin' the sun and heedin' the birds an' animals. They washed their claes, these folk, using soap they hid made theirsels wi' pron an' stale maister\* an' starched their claes wi' tatties.

Folk in Rafford used tae hold their markets in the kirkyaird in yon days an' used the flat stones for selling their wares."

Ma would always tut-tut under her breathe at this point but we thought it was funny.

"The wifies wi' their white mutches roon their heids wid be lined up vyin' wi' each ither tae sell their stockings an' plaidin', cheese an' butter an' ducks an' hens. Fit a racket there wid be wi' all these wifies shoutin' an' the ducks an' hens cacklin'. They wid stop an' tak a pinch o' snuff oot a box an' stairt rearrangin' their produce. Then the scraichin' an' roarin' wid start a' ower again. Folk wid come frae all aroon an' the menfolk wid tak tae nippin' here an' there when they heard someane hid whisky. There wis plenty whisky in yon days for the havin'. Most folk kent someane who hid a still and'could buy the stuff for a shilling a bottle. The woods aroon the Romach Loch wis well kent for distilling an' mony hooses were kent tae be smugglers' hames.

There were pedlars, of course, filthy chiels who lived on the moss most of the time an' wid try tae sell ye their peats. Doon frae the hills they wid come wi' their slow, rollin' step, tartan plaids ower their shooders an' their lang, lank, tangled hair hingin' doon their backs. Ye wid hae thocht Moses himsel' hid come tae dae business in Rafford!"

Ma would tut again and we would be set off giggling and laughing at the very thought of such a great and holy man coming to our part of the world.

"Loons sellin' sweeties wid come trundling up the road with sticks an' bits of cloth to catch the pennies that the Rafford laddies

---

\* bran and stale urine.

would throw at them in exchange for their wares. An' then Saunders Naemair wid wander by.

He wis a poor beggar man, Saunders, wha wid turn up frae time tae time. He hid rags on his back an' bits o' cloth rolled up in his hair. A harmless chiel, ye ken, but the local lads wid ask him,

'Fit's yer name, Saunders?'

'Saunders,' he wid say.

'Fit mair?'

'Naemair,' and off he wid trot tae find someane else to repeat the same thing tae.

There were nae auction mairts in yon days so if ye hid goods tae sell, ye jist set up yir stall an' got on wi'it yersel'.

The folk in Rafford, mind ye, didna always like the Dallas folk an' baith wid throw insults at each ither. Ah mind ma faither tellin' me that the Rafford men thocht the Dallas men were lyin' thieves an' they hid a tale to prove it.

There wis a mannie lived in Lennoch—Michael Grigor wis his name—an' he wis well kent as hivvin' tarry fingers. A neighbour of his missed a cairt ae day an' straicht awa went tae see Michael tae ask aboot it.

'Guid. Keep me fae stealin' such a big thing as a cairt!'

So the neighbour left.

Life must have got too much for Michael though for, not long efter that, he put himsel' into the Lossie at the pool now cried Michael's Pool. As he wis bein' cairried oot tae be buried, his neighbour leaned on the garden dyke, which gave way and fell wi' a clatter, revealin' not only the cairt but a ploo an' couters carefully built into the wa'."

We enjoyed the tale but couldn't for the life of us understand why Michael would go to the bother of stealing something like a cart just to hide it away and never use it. I suppose if something could be had for nothing without anyone knowing, then there were folk who would give it a go. The same happened with cattle. They were easy to lift and hard to prove whose they were.

"Dallas an' Rafford, of course, were on the edge of the Hielans whaur, folk said, most of the bairns grew up learnin' the ways o' the cattle rievers. Doon alang the Spey an' the Findhorn they wid come, often by the licht o' the Michaelmas moon—MacFarlane's lantern they cried it—leavin' their hovels in the west for the rich pickins ower Moray wye. The best-kent raid wis when the Grants made a descent into the glen o' the Lossie an' ravaged the land. Mony folk in the area, particularly aroon Kellas, were badly hit, losin' beasts, corn an' household goods. John Strachan's grandmither wis noted as haein' lost a silk goonie lined with tabbie (coarsely woven silk cloth) as weel as fifty poonds, pewter plates, tummlers an' three glass bottles full o' brandy an' aqua vitae. Fit wye the robbers cairried a' that withoot spillin' it's onyone's guess an' ah'm sure his grandmither sorely missed her drink. Sir Robert Gordon of Gordonstoun gaithered a few o' his retainers an' overtook the caterans on the hills above Knockando. Fit wis done tae them his been lost in the mists of time an' probably best left that wye."

"Richt, bairns, time for bed. Yir faither's weary wi' a' this tale-telling," Ma would say.

"Oh, Father, jist ane more story. Tell us aboot the penny weddin', please Father, jist the penny weddin'."

Our entreaties usually worked for Father enjoyed telling his stories as much as we enjoyed hearing them.

"The penny weddin', then, an' its off tae bed wi' ye all, mind."

We would snuggle into each other on the rag rug in front of the fire, each trying to get comfy on the hard floor. Father would begin.

"I mind ma granny tellin' me of how marriages were held when she wis a quine. No like they are noo, ye ken, but much simpler in some ways an' withoot the fuss o' fancy clothes an' the like. Because fermin' folk in yon days rarely hid a day off frae their never-endin' toil, they wid get thegither if there wis ony reason for a celebration. There wid be rejoicin' far an' near at happy family events an' holy days, older than the memories of even the oldest folk, wid be seen as good enough cause for festivities.

A new bairn's arrival in the world wis certainly worth celebratin' an' so, of course, wis a weddin'. When a young lad an' his lass wanted tae wed, there were certain things they hid tae see tae. First, there wis the 'bookin''—when the names o' the groom an' his betrothed were given to the session clerk, wha wis usually also the school-maister. As weel's his fees for proclaimin' the banns, the lad wha wis to be wed wid be asked for 'ba-money' for the bairns. If he refused, the loons in the school hid the richt tae meet the bride as she left the kirk an' rin off wi' her sheen. They wid only gie them back ance they got their money. Then, three weeks afore the weddin', the groom an' his best man an' the bride an' her bridesmaid called on their freens an' invited them tae come. This wis cried the 'biddin'.' No letters, mind. Aabody hid tae be asked in person.

Ance these formalities were seen tae, the couple an' their freens could concentrate on the celebration itsel'. An' fit a palaiver it proved tae be.

The nicht afore the marriage, freens of the bride an' groom met in each hoose an', amidst great rejoicin' an caperin', they began smearin' their legs wi' grease frae the kitchen an' soot frae the lum. All the while, they wid be fillin' their glesses frae the tappit hen sittin' in the corner."

Ma would always tut at that bit, for she knew the story as well as my father did and didn't really approve of all that drinking.

"In the bride's hoose, a muckle wooden tub wid be found an' she wid be made tae stan in it while her freens set aboot washin' her feet. Into the lather, someane wid throw a weddin' ring an' all her freens, loons an' quines, wid scramble an' guddle in the soapy water until some lucky bodie found the ring. This wis a wonderful thing for they were sure tae be mairrit within the year."

Meg and I would nudge each other and laugh.

"The next day, the bridal party set off for the manse in twa separate processions. The bride hid twa loons wi' her an' the rest o' the company followed three by three—ae quine an' twa loons then twa quines an' ae loon a' so on. A horse an' cairt wi' the bride's plenishings, her chest of drawers an' store o' linen followed at the back. Whaever the bridal party met first alang the road—no matter be it gentry or plooman or how big a hurry they were in—they were bound tae stop an' drink a gless o' whisky to the prosperity of the bride frae a bottle which ane o' the loons cairried wi' him. This wis cried 'first footin' an' the same custom wis observed by the groom's pairty.

Ance the meenister hid mairrit them an' they hid done wi' a' the kirkin' business," (another tut from Ma !), "the bride an' groom wi' their freens wid process on foot to their future hame led by a piper playin' some bonny tune or ither. Jist afore they reached the hoose, the young men formed a line to run the keal. This wis naethin' more than a race an' the winner could claim his prize of the first kiss of the bride afore she entered her new hame. When the bridal pairty reached the homestead they found it surrounded by a' their neebours and freens, wha fired off pistols an' guns, waved flags an' scrambled for coppers as it approached. At the doorway, an auld wifie stood waitin' wi' a plate o' bride's cake in her haun, which she crumbled an' threw ower the bride as she crossed the threshold. As mony folk as could were squeezed an' squashed into the hoose. The rest were taken into ony nearby barn or cottage whaur a space wis found for them a'.

Well, efter a' that palaiver, aabody wis richt hungry so as mony as could get tae the table sat down for the weddin' feast. An' fit a spread there wis! Broth wi' shreds o' meat an' fowl boiled in't would start them off, then boiled an' roast meat wi' neeps a' tatties an' all washed doon wi' muckle tummlers o' whisky. When aabody hid eaten their fill, twa men, wha hid been picked as managers of the feast went roon the company carrying a plate to collect the 'lawin'' which wis always 1/- a head. In yon days, a Scots shilling wis the same as a penny an' every lad paid for his lass as weel's himsel'.

As soon as dinner wis ower, the bridegroom took his new wife by the haun an' led her tae the green in front o' the hoose tae dance the 'shamit' reel. The best mannie wid come rushin forrit an' claim her as his partner. The bridegroom then chose the bridesmaid tae dance wi'. The best man asked the bride fit wis tae be 'the shame spring'. She wis tae answer, 'through the warld will I gang wi' the lad that lo'es me'. Then the music struck up an' the dancin' stairted, the rest o the company lookin' on in silence until it finished, when aabody clapped an' clapped for the newly mairried pair.

All that day an' well into the evenin' the dancin' an' drinkin' continued. Ony of the lads wha chose to gie the fiddlers a halfpenny could hae his favourite tune played. He then chose the quine he wished tae honour an' took the floor wi' her. As mony ither couples as the room could hold were allowed tae jyne in the dance. Efter the fiddlers hid played the tune ower aboot a dizzen times, they paused. The lads cried oot 'kissin' time' an' proceeded tae kiss their pairtners. The tune wis played ance or twice mair an' the dance ended.

By this time, aabody wis needin' tae get some rest so the last thing tae be done wis tae see tae the beddin' of the young couple an' the ceremony of throwin' the stockin'. This wis the most excitin' part of the whole evening, for, whaever managed tae get hold of the bride's stockin' when she took it off wis sure tae be the next bride or groom in the place.

The third day of the celebrations were devoted to eatin', drinkin' an' haein' fun. On the evening of that day those folk wha hid lang distances to go wid set off for hame. But, on the fourth day, which wis aye a Sunday, as mony of the young couples' freens wha were still there an' were nae too tired, accompanied them to the kirk.

An' that wis the end of the penny weddin'."

By the time he had finished, Sandy and Meg would be asleep but I loved hearing that story and could have listened to Father telling it every night if he had the mind to.

# Chapter 14

# Loosening Strings

Father would run sheep on our hill for another farmer over the winter and that would keep us occupied too. Any fencing that needed repaired had to be seen to even if the ground was frozen and the biting north wind was blowing hard. The drains and ditches had to be cleared and, of course, the cows, hens and pigs all had to be fed and watered.

Winters were often severe in our parts. It was not unknown for snow to lie ten or even twenty feet deep, making any movement about the place impossible. The bracing, cold air was thought to be fortifying and good for your health and many an old person credited their long lives to the keen, invigorating breezes that blew in all directions through Dallas. One winter in particular, I remember opening the door of the house to find snow up to my shoulders.

"Ye canna gyang tae the school the day, Molly. Naething's movin' wi' sae muckle snaw."

Father went to shut the door.

"But, Faither, ah'll lose ma perfect attendance. A hiv tae gang."

I would not be dissuaded and my poor father had to get the shovel out and cut a path from the door to the road.

Our bonnie corner o' Moray lay silent that morning. My feet were snugly laced into their black boots with steel heels and tackets hammered through the soles. I was aye gey hard on my boots with all the scratching and scraping that I put them through and if they lasted till spring, I did well. When the soles were worn through I would line them with cardboard to extend their life a bit and then, as soon as the warmer weather came, they would be discarded for sandshoes—or no shoes at all.

Slowly and laboriously I slithered and slipped the three miles, past the house where Winnie MacKay and her family bided, past Rhininver where my father grew up and up the brae to the school. By the roadside, all was still save for the drips from the overhanging trees, pockmarking the snow on the ground and showering me with dustings of powder or dollops of ice. I was now the only quine left at home and no longer needed to share my hat with Meg. One by one, my sisters had gone and now only Sandy and I were left at home. Meg had followed the rest to Forres and was busy keeping house for Auntie Annie.

In the winter, the wind would often come from the north-east and it could cut through you to your very marrow. With teeth clenched and eyes shut at times, the head would go down and the shoulders up as the wind stung my cheeks and tried its best to blow me away across the fields. I was well happit, though. Vest and knickers, liberty bodice from which dangled loops with tapes attached to the top of my thick, full-length, woollen stockings, heavy jumper and serge skirt were all encased inside a warm coat. A cosy bonnet and woollen gloves completed the outfit. I was as snug as any bug, either in a rug or those under my semmit.

Once the safety of the school was reached, all the wet coats and boots would be peeled off and draped around the fire. A steaming mug of cocoa would warm our innards before lessons began.

Although Christmas was not celebrated in a big way, any excuse to break the monotony of lessons was eagerly grasped we made the most of it. I was now in the headmaster's class for the third and last year. Singing had to be practised and memorised for the concert we were to put on for parents and neighbours. 'Alice Blue Gown' was the chosen piece and we lined up every afternoon to practise and practise and better than practise. Of course, Alice Garrow stood in front of me and it would not have right if, each time we sang 'Alice', I didn't poke her in the back with my finger. To give her her due, she put up with it for some time before finally complaining. Needless to say, I was strapped but am the first to admit that, on this occasion, I probably deserved it.

The Christmas play was put on every year in the Institute and was a tradition that the senior class each year was called on to uphold. In my last Christmas as a pupil, I was the 'child' to Eva MacKenzie's 'mother.' I've no recollection what the play was about but do remember my role entailed rocking the baby in its makeshift cradle and being told by 'mother' to go out for more coal.

Obviously, I wasn't meant to be happy about this for my instructions were to start crying, which I did with volume and gusto. I should add that, while off stage I had applied soot to my face to prove that I had been at the coal box but, not having a mirror, I plastered it on so thickly and over every inch of my face, that I was crying real tears when I re-entered with the smarting of my eyes.

"Gie's a towel, Ma, I canna see!"

The well- practised line was delivered with genuine pathos and not a little urgency and I hope the audience, including Ma, appreciated the quality of the acting. I scrubbed my face till I almost drew blood but still had traces of black at the party held afterwards.

The Houldsworths were very generous to the folk in the village and surrounding area. Not only had they gifted us a handsome hall in which to hold meetings, whists, games and the like, they also provided a tree each year, decorated with baubles, balloons and streamers for our party. They made sure that whichever Santa had been coerced into service had a present for every child in the parish — a wee book or game just, but enough to make the day special for us. That year, I mind I got a game of Ludo and thought it was the best present ever. After the party, I even got to stay the night with Eva, which was a rare treat for us both.

In winter, Whooper swans and Greylag geese would take up residence in the hill lochs that were strewn around Branchill. They would arrive from the north—Iceland, Father would tell us—and stay until the weather started to warm up again. I loved the heavy beat of their wings as they flew overhead. When the laverock returned to bewitch us with its soaring aerial display and clear song, we knew that spring could not be far away. And when the sun began to rise higher in the sky, so too did our beloved peewits. They were aye there, the peesies, as much a sound of home as the gales lifting the rafters in the barn or the wind moaning and complaining in the lum.

Because I was the only girl left at home now, Ma would take me with her to basket whists in the village. And great fun they were, too. All the women-folk would take milk, sugar and tea along with eats of some kind, most likely girdle scones or pancakes. The fun we would have at these whists was grand. I mind on one occasion being at Menzies Mill and once the cards were put away, the mothers all went home and the youngsters had the place to themselves to have a dance. I canna mind where the music came from or how many folk were there but I do mind thinking if this is what its like being a grown-up, then I canna wait. Already, subtle changes to my body were beginning to alter my shape and turn me away from childish notions and games.

We had concerts and the like in the Institute from time to time. Dallas boasted an accordion band in those days and very good it was, too. We also had dances in the hall with music from fiddle and melodeon provided by folk that you never expected could play such things and bothy ballads sung enthusiastically by everyone in the hall. Social occasions, grand and small, cemented our far-flung community.

Folk had a get-together when there was any excuse and sometimes when there was none. The staff at Grangehall, where Annie worked, had a party one winter's evening and Meg and I were invited. I must have been fourteen or so but remember not enjoying myself. My deafness prevented me joining in conversations and excluded me to a large extent from the fun and joking. A chicken bone got stuck in my throat that night, too, and I mind coming home in the butcher's van the next morning and sleeping the whole way. I was beginning to realise that not being able to hear very well was going to shut me out in social gatherings. And so it has proved throughout my life. I made up my mind at that point that I would have to find other ways to entertain myself.

A regular bus service had begun to ply between Forres and Elgin since the late twenties and came through Dallas in the summer. Hendry MacDonald had set up in business from the Palace Garage in South Street in Elgin and his two green buses could be seen making their way along the road, stopping wherever a wifie wanted on or a parcel was to be dropped off. Everything was carried on the bus—bikes, batteries for wireless sets and boxes of groceries from the town, all accompanied by the odd oath or two from the driver when the engine stalled and he had to get out to crank it back into life with the starting handle.

Stories would be told of the times in the winter when, if it was very cold, the water had to be drained from the engines at night and filled up again in the morning with warm water carried in pails from Austin's Bakery. They were more than bus drivers these men who brought the outside world to Dallas and took its young people away. They were all larger than life characters who were loved like family by the villagers and, many years later, one of the best-loved, Bobby Green, was honoured, on his retirement, by the folk of Dallas for his faithful service to the community. 'Bobby's bus' has a special place in many folks' hearts.

The summer term in school was always busy. In my last year, it was even more so. The 'qualifying' exam had been sat and passed but I couldn't look forward to going on to the Academy like Winnie and the others. Domestic work was to be my lot and I already knew from my sisters that a hard lot it would be. But there was still fun to be had and, though I knew the time was coming to put away childish things, I was determined to enjoy my last days at school.

The sports were held every year in the field behind the playground. Parents and friends came along to watch and brought picnics with them. The whole day was like a carnival and, of course, we had races. Ma had always said I was swack on my feet and so I was. Running five miles every day to school and back had made me light on my feet and as lean and fast as the roe deer that sometimes startled us along the green road. Ma had come to watch and it was one of the highlights of my young days to run against the whole school and come first with my proud mother watching. At least, I hope she was proud. She never said.

I was so pleased too, that Alice Garrow and I won the three-legged race that day. We had practised and practised our technique until we ran in exact unison with each other, our 'joined' leg hitting the ground with a regular rhythm and each hauling the other over the ground until the tape was reached.

The school always had a summer picnic to the seaside at either Lossiemouth or Nairn as a treat at the end of term. I always got new sandshoes for the picnic but they were cast aside for races. I still liked running in my bare feet. Miles of sand and sparkling sea would mean we had plenty to do, running races, paddling in the water and daring each other to go in over our knees. Sandwiches, buns, cakes and lemonade ensured we were never hungry, though, by the time we were on our way home, we would be looking for something else to eat.

Magical days in a crowded bus, full of chattering, happy voices, balloons and streamers escaping from open windows and faces burnt with sun and glowing with the joy of one another's friendship.

All along the Moray Firth are dotted small villages that, all too often are at the mercy of the elements. There is nowhere more serenely beautiful than the North Sea when the day is settled and its benign waters lap gently, sighing on the sand. Neither is there anywhere more terrifyingly hostile and malevolent than the same sea, roaring and growling its anger and menacing the folk who live in the villages along its shore.

One of these villages was Culbin, which suffered a catastrophe as awful for the folk there as that in far away Pompeii long ago. It was not ash and lava that blocked out the sun forever in Culbin, but sand—the same sand that we played on and dug our bare toes into generations later. Sand storms were not unknown in these parts and varied in strength and intensity. The one that struck Culbin in the autumn of 1694 came from the west suddenly and without any warning. Workers in the field, harvesting a crop of late barley had to abandon their work and farmers ploughing their fields for next year's planting were forced to stop their plough in mid furrow. Within a matter of hours, plough and crop were under the sand, which had spread its menace stealthily and ruthlessly, drifting and accumulating in great mounds and choking field after field.

Nothing was spared.

The wind, gaining in strength and ferocity, whipped the sand over the simple homes of the villagers, seeking out every nook, cranny, crevice and corner, sparing neither rich man nor poor. In brutal gusts, it laid waste the entire community, smothering orchard and lawn, cottage and castle. By the morning, the winds had abated. The villagers were forced to break out through the backs of their houses to rescue their bellowing, terrified cattle and lead them to safety. No sooner had they done that but the wind whipped up again, screaming and wailing like a tortured soul, hurling sand in all directions. The terrified people had to flee for their lives, leaving everything they possessed.

The swirling storm choked fields and farms and smothered the mouth of the Findhorn, which was then forced to find a new opening to the sea. It spewed its peaty waters over previously cultivated land drowning cattle and crops and left behind pools and lakes where before none had existed. In the course of its rage, it swept to oblivion the village at its mouth and many of the souls in it.

When the fury died away and the people returned, not a trace could be found of their homes. All traces of habitation had been obliterated and everything was swathed in sand.

Folk, even today, find a visit to Culbin an eerie experience and some claim to have seen the old mansion house re-appear from time to time, only to sink again beneath the dunes. There's an unearthly silence over the sands there to this day and I, for one, would not like to find myself alone there on a stormy night. When I was a bairn, there were many who would not set foot on the place.

Nor would they yet.

# Chapter 15

# Away Beyond the Green Road

My last days at Dallas School passed in a rush of finishing off and packing away. The friends I had sat beside and confided in for what seemed a lifetime, were to scatter to the four corners and, in their keeping, my youth and innocence. The last event of the school year was always the prize-giving, when the accumulation of marks gained and tests passed were totted up to ascertain the pupils who merited prizes. I had regularly received firsts and seconds throughout my school career but was still delighted to be told that I had won the dux prize.

The ceremony was held in the school itself and, though Ma couldn't come, Bella promised she would bring Sandy to watch me receiving my award. All morning, I watched the door and waited but there was no sign of either of them. I was duly presented with my book, prize for perfect attendance and Leaving Certificate but felt a stab of sadness that none of my family had been there to share the moment with me.

I could hear the greetin' before I walked into the house.

Bella and Sandy had set off right enough on Bella's bike with Sandy given dire warnings to keep his feet well away from the wheels. Of course he forgot and ended up on the ground with Bella and the bike on top of him and a goodly amount of skin missing from his ankle. It must have been gey painful for the bawlin' and greetin' went on for hours. Every so often, face down on the bed, he would stop for breath and then work up to a grander roar, as if to emphasis the extent of his suffering.

In the room across the landing, Bella was face down on her bed, too, sobbing fit tae burst for not looking after her wee brother the way a sister should and causing him so much anguish. They lay there, in adjacent misery, crying and wailing until exhaustion overcame them and they succumbed to sleep.

Sandy's leg took many weeks to heal and he only needed to catch a glimpse of the nurse on her bike a mile away, coming to change his dressing, for the roaring to start up again. After a while, no one came running and even the hens, now his only audience, stopped heeding his uproar and carried on with their pecking and scraping.

On that last summer's day, walking home along the green road, I knew that nothing would ever be the same again. My childhood was over and the friends that I valued beyond riches would no longer be part of my world. The parents and brother whom I loved so much would remain at home but they would soon only know me as a visitor. The sisters I worshipped were already establishing their own independent lives and increasingly pulling away from us. Our family ties were strong, though, and would bind us together wherever we went. I was sure of that.

Bella had been working for some time at the Boat of Garten, a small village between Grantown-on -Spey and Aviemore. Jean and I were to join her in the summer I was 15, Jean to work in the Manse and me to help Bella. The house she worked in was called Monaliadh.

Could we say it? We tied our tongues in knots and twisted our tonsils trying to pronounce it. It was our first encounter with Gaelic!

The family she worked for were the Grants, who ran not only the local grocer's shop but also a drapery with a tearoom upstairs. Bella had all the linen to launder from the tearoom as well as running the house for the family. There were three sons, all of whom were at university in Edinburgh. At least one was training to be a doctor and all needed clean white shirts every day. So, twice a week, a parcel containing soiled laundry would arrive by train from Edinburgh to be washed, dried and ironed ready to catch the early train south next day. Poor Bella. She always had the lion's share of the work to do but she never complained.

Mr. Grant had, for a reason unknown to us, lost his nerve for driving, preferring to hire a car should the need arise. During the summer holidays, his sons didn't want to be stuck at home and, with 'The Boat' being relatively remote and only having the occasional train to rely on, it was suggested that Bella should learn to drive. This was 1935, when the few cars that were about were almost exclusively driven by men. That didn't bother Bella. Once her work was over for the day, she would take herself off to the big shed which housed the car and spend many hours practising gear changing and acquainting herself with the pedals. Eventually, she felt confident enough to venture on to the driveway and, when no-one was about, would steer the beast between the clumps of vegetation growing alongside the road and get used to the feel and weight of the contraption.

The gardener was an old fellow who lived some miles from the house and he had to walk back and forward to work every day. I'm not sure how Bella managed to persuade him to get into the car, wary as he was of new-fangled machines, but off they went, she gripping the wheel till her knuckles near burst out of their skin and he gripping the door handle with the same intensity and his face the colour of putty. She got him safely home but had the dickens of a job turning the car while managing heroically not to get the wheels stuck in the mud.

Bella continued to drive all over the Highlands until well into her eighties without accident, only reluctantly relinquishing her car when her eyesight deteriorated. She never sat a test—she was never required to—but could proved her ability to anyone who was brave enough to question it!

The Grants also had a bungalow in their grounds that they let out in the summer. It was here that I was put to work cleaning for a maiden lady and her housekeeper from Hillhead in Glasgow. I enjoyed the work and the Grants were good to me. It was most agreeable to be getting paid for something that was second nature to me. I never felt homesick. I had my sisters nearby.

My second summer at the Boat was not such an enjoyable one. I found myself working as scullery maid in the Hotel, under the 'tutelage' of the kitchen maid. She was 20—only four years older than me! Naturally, I was given the hardest and lowliest work to do —scrubbing floors and washing all the dishes as well as the numerous pots which had to be descaled with metal scourers. Long hours and little sleep turned a healthy, robust lassie into a pale and drawn craitur as I struggled to keep up with the never-ending piles waiting for me in the sink. Eventually, my health deteriorated so much that my fingers became poisoned and the cysts had to be lanced by the doctor. The infection had spread right up my arms and attacked the glands under my oxters. Sympathy was rarely shown and never expected but even the coldest heart would surely be minded to care for the fledgeling skivvy. Not a bit of it! I was not allowed to get my hands wet so the housemaid had to take on my job of washing. She was not happy and each time I dried a plate, she would plunge it into the sink again out of badness and I would have to dry it for a second or even third time. My fingers took weeks to heal because of her malice and cruelty. The only comfort I had was, years later, hearing that she had suffered the same fate with her fingers when she went to work in London. I hope she got the same treatment from her employer as I got from her!

## Chapter 16

## Tchaikovsky and Chamberlain

My father's health had been slowly getting worse and by the harvest of 1936, he was admitted to Leanchoil Hospital. His heart was failing and years of malnourishment and hard work had left him weak and unable to fight on. They took all his teeth out—not that he had many left—and, in a week, he had shrunk and become a very old man. The family had been called for and took turns in visiting him.

The first night home, I cycled down to see him. It was windy and I had wrapped my flapping coat over my knees. Only it wasn't over my knees—it was over the handlebars. I catapulted over the front wheel with my much-abused chin making initial contact with the ground and losing another layer of skin on Rafford Brae. What a mess I was in! I had to go to Auntie Annie to be cleaned up before I could present myself at the hospital.

While he was a patient, the matron had asked him if he any of his daughters could work as a domestic. Being the only one without a regular job, I was volunteered, which is why I found myself shortly after walking through the imposing doors of Leanchoil Hospital in Forres for my first full-time job. I was 16.

Father got home but we all knew he didn't have long. We watched him slowing down to a shuffle with the smallest movement becoming an ordeal for him. One of the last memories I have of my beloved father was the painful sight of him trying to get up from his chair to go to the privy behind the byre last thing at night.

Annie and Bella had come home to be with him and had sat by his bedside during the long, cold nights of his dying. They didn't notice that he had slipped away at first. His breathing had become softer and lighter until it just stopped altogether. He left us as he had lived, gently and with dignity, in the early hours of Armistice Day in his 64th year.

The open coffin lay in 'the room' until the funeral. Mr. Matheson the minister conducted the service and all our neighbours and friends crowded into the tiny parlour. Afterwards, the men took turns to carry the coffin the three miles from Branchill to the kirkyard, where they laid Robbie to rest under the shelter of the north wall and within sound of the gentle Lossie.

I remember little of the funeral except Auntie Nellie holding my hand. What a special person she was to us all—a lady who had suffered the loss of her own two wee girls but whose great capacity for love shone through as she comforted a bewildered child.

After the burial, I was sent to the village for bread. On the way home, I found myself going through the graveyard to look at the newly filled grave with the solitary family wreath lying on top of the replaced turfs.

"Were ye no feart gyan tae the kirkyerd on yer ain?" speired Sandy, who was only 11.

I lived in my own silent world most of the time and hadn't picked up on anything to be afraid of. I suppose being deaf acts as a filter to other folks' apprehensions and fears but also their joys and excitement. They're very much infectious emotions.

All our neighbours rallied round Ma, but there was no question of her being able to stay at Branchill. She had not only lost her man and provider but would lose the home they had shared for over twenty years. She couldn't have coped with the croft on her own anyway and, with Sandy still at school and the rest of us away working, she had to leave.

She was offered a farm cottage at Blackhillock, just over the hill but out of sight of Branchill and stayed there until she got a house in the village and the job of cleaning the school. All the farm implements and many of the household furnishings had to be sold. A roup was organised and Bella minds painting the wheels of the cart to brighten them up. I never got the chance to claim any of Ma's china as I was working on the day of the roup—something I regret still. She didn't have much that was worth selling but the few dishes she had were bonny and precious.

I don't remember particularly my first day at the hospital but I'm sure I would have been set to work right away by Matron Ross. I was to share a room with the ward maid, Margaret McStephen, who was to become one of my dearest and most abiding friends. The new nurses' home was still in the process of being built so we had a room on the top floor of the hospital. We were wakened at 6 a.m. and started work half an hour later. There was no breakfast until the long corridor had been swept from the back door to the front and the doorstep whitened with London Stone.

I was responsible for all the corridors and the Matron's and nurses' sitting rooms. Most of the time I was on my knees with nothing between them and the cold linoleum floor. And my but they got stiff and sore with all that kneeling! All the polishing had to be done by hand then removed and buffed with a machine we called a dummy. It had bristles for applying the polish and a cloth underneath for buffing. It was very heavy and needed careful handling if it wasn't to take off on its own and Palais Glide down the passage. Once I had mastered its idiosyncrasies, life became a lot easier and I soon adopted the push with one hand, retrieve with the other method, which enabled the beast to carry out its duties without disabling me.

We had our breakfast when Matron did her ward rounds and were very fortunate to be at Leanchoil when Mary Barron was cook. She fed us well and made tea and scones for us after our cleaning duties were done for the day. Then we put on long white aprons and caps to serve Matron's and Sister's breakfasts. Once we had cleared and tidied their rooms, we had lunch before changing into a black dress and cap for our afternoon duties. We would usually have a few hours off around 3 o'clock but had to be back to serve the patients' supper around 5. Our day finished about 9p.m. We had one half day per week and every second Sunday off. Our half-day started at 3 o'clock!

When the new nurses' home was finished, Margaret and I shared a bedroom, sitting room and bathroom. We had central heating and overlooked the golf course. The luxury of having all that space was only surpassed by having a wardrobe EACH! At home, my wardrobe was a nail on the back of the door. Now I had an enormous closet to call my own. Never mind that I had few clothes to hang in it, I was ecstatic.

Margaret and I were so proud of our rooms that we both worked hard at keeping them immaculate. One afternoon when we were having a break, Margaret heard the Matron's voice on the stairs. She pushed me into my wardrobe and disappeared into her own.

Matron was showing a visitor round the staff quarters and proclaimed on opening the bedroom door,

"I'm not afraid to show anybody these rooms. They belong to our two most conscientious members of staff."

I could feel my lugs glowing but was secretly flattered that she felt that way. She was a lady who expected the highest standard of cleanliness from everyone and made sure she got it. From that moment, I endeavoured to always give my best effort, no matter how menial the task.

One other luxury in our room was a gramaphone. I had never owned such a thing although I had heard dance music played on one at Caldhame. And we had a record. It was Tchaikovsky's 1812 Overture, which I found incredibly rousing—I'd never heard classical music and played it so often and so loud you would have expected Napoleon himself to be at the gates of Forres.

Margaret was my ears for much of the time and got me into situations I wouldn't have found myself in on my own. Our room was on the ground floor and it wasn't long before we would climb out of the window and make off for Forres to have a mooch about and meet up with other lads and quines. We had to have permission to be out after work and were usually allowed to go to dances in the villages around Forres. We had to be back by 10. You can have a lot of fun in a couple of hours and I really enjoyed these first few years of adult life and revelled in my independence.

I was always too shy to go out with boys but Margaret was already going with Bert who would eventually become her husband. She once fixed me up with a blind date to make up a foursome. When he turned up, the poor loon had a patch over one eye but as we were going to the pictures, I felt no one would see us. Of course, I couldn't hear a word he said to me as I couldn't read his lips in the dark and when we came out, I took to my heels, leaving the lad wondering what was going on. It wasn't me being deliberately unkind, I just felt scared at not being in control when I couldn't hear. That feeling has been with me all my life and, sadly, not knowing the circumstances, other folk have misunderstood my apparent aloofness and detachment.

Eventually, I started going to dances with a lad, Tom, from Brodie and must have liked him well enough for we got engaged. A ring with sapphires and diamonds, it was. I was 18 and barely knew what life was about. When he had the ring on my finger he assumed he would be entitled to all the perks but I wasn't that naïve and ended our relationship. I canna even mind his second name now so that tells you of the depth of feelings I had for the poor loon. I don't mind love being much of an issue in these days for marriage. If you liked someone well enough and he liked you, you just made a go of it. If it worked out well, that was a bonus. Often, it didn't and that was just your hard luck.

I earned £1.17.6d per calendar month and that had to pay for everything. Out of my earnings, I managed to save enough to buy my first bike. It cost £12 and took nearly two years to save for it. I didn't like buying anything I couldn't afford to pay outright—and still don't. I would rather do without than owe anyone any money. The bike was so handy for getting home on my days off and I loved getting back to catch up with Ma and the others if they were there. I also managed to buy a Brownie box camera and, every month, spent 1/- on a film and another to have it developed. That camera captured many precious moments of my early life and I still have a greet to myself when I look at the dear faces that were so precious to me.

When I decided to look for a better-paid job, the local Labour Exchange found me one at Trinity College, Glenalmond, a boys' fee-paying school near Crieff. Bella, by this time was married to Sandy McCabe and was living in Auchterarder. She had just had her first child, Ishbel, and I was anxious to be near her to help out when I could. My work was to be in the sanitorium of the boys' school—the sick bay to us.

Trinity College was founded by William Gladstone, James Hope-Scott and Dean Ramsay in 1847, primarily as a school and seminary for boys entering the ministry of the Scottish Episcopal Church. Up until the year before I moved there, all the wardens had been clergymen. It was home to sons of foreign diplomats, army officers and anyone who could afford to give their offspring a private education. There were all sorts there from a wide range of backgrounds but as I worked in the sick bay, saw them only when illness or disease equalled them all as patients.

Sister Robertson met me by car at Perth railway station and drove me to my new home. She told me later that, when she saw me stepping from the train, she said to herself 'that one will stay for a while.' My bike had travelled third class in the guard's van and was stashed in a shed until I could arrange for it to be collected.

Trinity College was an imposing structure, built round a quadrangle with a variety of outbuildings. The sick bay stood some distance away. We were never inundated with customers unless there was an outbreak of an infectious disease or galloping virus. Most of the time, Agnes, the other maid, and I helped Sister Robertson and performed any duty that was required of us—cleaning, cooking, filling the water buckets and cutting logs for the fire. There was an Aga in the kitchen, which had to be cleaned morning and night and a coal fire in the sitting-room, so we were very comfortable. I was certainly well looked after and very content, always whistling away to myself. I now realise that because I couldn't hear myself, I would be whistling louder than was appropriate and mind being asked by sister to stop whistling as the doctor couldn't hear his patient's heart beat!

As I say, we coped well until there was an epidemic. I mind many of the boys took German Measles and filled the sanitorium to capacity. I also took the disease but was not allowed to stay off. I had to continue serving food to the boys though I was feeling gey sick myself. Eventually, two other girls were brought in to help out. They hailed from Glasgow and were a bit rough and different to the kind of folk I had met up till then.

On the few occasions I had any time off I would cycle to see Bella or go to dances and badminton in the village halls round about. It was around this time that I met Bob, who became my second fiancé. He was a very quiet lad and lodged with a friend of mine, Mrs. Kay, who occasionally helped out in the sick-bay if we were busy. We didn't really have a lot in common. I was still only in my teens and I don't expect I really wanted to settle down at that stage of my life. But he bought me a lovely ring, more sapphires and diamonds, and we, I suppose, were happy enough.

One afternoon, when I was up in my room having a break, the two Glasgow girls burst in and, before I knew what was happening, started to pull my clothes off and touch me in places no-one had ever touched me before.

"Let's see what you've been showing this Bob of yours!" they sniggered as one held me down while the other tore at my underclothes. I screamed and kicked and managed to right myself, running into the bathroom and locking the door.

I was in a right old state, shaking and sobbing uncontrollably and stayed there for over an hour.

The next day, I was down on my knees, cleaning out a cupboard in the kitchen when Sister Robertson passed behind me.

"You've a good pair of legs on you, Molly. It must be all that cycling."

I never replied but stood up and turned to face her.

"My goodness, what's wrong with you, my dear? You look as if you haven't slept all night."

It was the caring tone of her voice and her kindness to me since I had started there that opened the floodgates and out the whole sorry story came. When I had finished telling her what had happened, she went to her office, summoned the two girls and dismissed them on the spot—without pay or references and leaving them to find their own way to the station.

My working day usually started at 7.30. and finished at 7p.m. with a break of a few hours in the afternoon. Bella had now moved into Perth (the third of more than twenty flittings Bella had to endure throughout her life!). On my afternoon off, I would cycle to Glenalmond and catch the bus for Perth. It was while she was there that I lost my top teeth! Pyorrhoea had set into my gums and coaxed all the teeth to leave their sockets. The dentist took them all out, without anaesthetic, and I stayed with Bella for two or three days to recover.

September came in much like any other month in 1939 but before it was out, life for me and those around me had changed forever. When Neville Chamberlain delivered his address to the nation on $3^{rd}$ of that month, many's a door closed behind him—including the door of my innocence and carefree youth.

## Chapter 17

## Cassocks and Bare Feet

If the start of war heralded the end of my youth, more than two hundred miles away other lives were also being stolen and reshaped. From every clachan and town, village and island, the Territorial army was being assembled as part of the first wave of the British Expeditionary Force. Part of that army was a man called Johnny—a man I didn't yet know but whose life was to become part of mine before the decade was out.

It wasn't easy being pupil 5666 on the admission register of Rockfield Road School when you had nothing to wear on your feet and you were always hungry.

Johnny Livingstone was five and had now acquired his second number. The first was on his birth certificate which declared that he had opened his eyes to the world in Shore Street in Oban on 1$^{st}$July1906. His sister, Mary, was three.

Life was hard for the family. Granny had to take in other folk's washing to supplement her meagre resources and was responsible for bringing up her daughter's children while she sought work in the city. Granny was a widow and there was little money for food or clothes. Her husband John had a pittance of a pension from his time in the army and, when he died suddenly from gallstones, she got the 2/6d back from the return of his porter's badge. And that was about it. She had been left with three young children to raise on her own and had done the best with what little she had. Now the next generation had begun arriving and she had to start all over again.

Duncanina McNiven had come to work in Oban in the 1880's from Ballachulish and had met and married John Livingstone, recently retired from the Argyll Volunteers.

He had bought the badge that authorised him to operate as a porter, carrying travellers' luggage from train and coach to the many new hotels springing up along the Corran Esplanade. Fate dealt the young family a cruel blow when, after only seven years together, John died. His widow was left with James, Mary and Hughina, only an infant, to struggle on alone.

Now, with her daughter ill and two young mouths to feed, she had to take in other people's washing to put food on the table and clothes on their backs. Young Mary and Johnny went barefoot from spring 'til autumn when a timely grant each September from the Association for Improving the Conditions of the Poor ensured they had boots for the winter. Such poverty was the normal way of life for many children at the beginning of the 20$^{th}$ century.

If material comforts were lacking, there was an endless supply of love and support from Granny and an extended family, whose roots were in the lands of Mull, Morvern and Appin. Visits by big Auntie Annie MacAskill would find Johnny running for cover to avoid her over-enthusiastic and suffocating hugs and kisses.

'Far an robh mi'n raoir' and 'Gleann Bhaile Chaoil' would soothe him to sleep every night. By the time he started school in 1911, his mother Mary was being wracked by the consumptive cough which would take her life seven years later.

Rockfield Road School housed the infant and junior sections of Oban High School of which William Kennedy was Rector. Alexander Faichney was in charge at Rockfield and under him a battalion of spinster teachers. Miss Fraser, Miss Rankin and Miss Hope, amongst others, strove to mould and educate their charges. Pencils on slates shaped their early numbers and letters and Mr. Nisbet, the music master, gave singing lessons.

They were exhorted to take part in Swedish Drill with Miss Borthwick on Fridays and the infants, in particular, apparently 'liked paper tearing'. Periodically, the Rector would examine his charges and declare himself, in general, pleased with their progress.

Infectious diseases like chickenpox, measles and ringworm resulted in a dramatic fall in attendance from time to time, as did stormy or particularly wet weather. Without adequate clothing, most of the poorer pupils simply stayed at home.

Every Friday, the class with the best attendance for the week got 'The Banner'—a reward entitling them to leave school early. For those who remained, the janitor would invariably recount tales of the Boer War and re-enact the Siege of Mafeking with brandished sword and martial fervour. The children knew to keep their heads down. Argyll County Council must have queried, though, the regular replacement of light fittings in that classroom but for Johnny and his classmates, the excitement of Friday afternoons were a fitting overture to their weekends, when soldiering and war would be played out in their own games in the lanes and car-free streets of the town.

Out of school, Johnny would also amuse myself with his pals, racing each other round 'The Moyle'—a rectangle comprising Argyll Street, Tweeddale Street, Stevenson Street and George Street. If the milk or coal cart had just passed by, pulled by one of the docile Clydesdale horses, a favourite game would be to jump into the newly deposited pats on the road. That was good for warming up cold toes. Street games like kick the can or hide and seek were played, as was football if a ball could be found. If you lived in Tweeddale Street like Johnny did, the blacksmith's workshop, distillery and gasworks all added their particular sounds and smells to your world.

Granny had brought with her to Oban her Episcopalian faith and both Mary and Johnny were baptised at the onyx and marble font in St John's Cathedral. The children were musical and Johnny was soon able to earn a few pennies as a choir boy in the church. Under the tutelage of Mr. Frank Saunders a school-master, Johnny would practise twice a week and sing for real at Sunday Services, funerals and Church Festivals. The ragged clothes and bare feet he wore for the rest of the week was in marked contrast to the starched Eton collar, red cassock and white linen surplice he donned on Sundays and his regular attendance at St John's must have acted as a leveller to him with his fellow choristers, many of whom were sons of lawyers, clerics and bank managers. At least he glimpsed a hint of a better life once a week and must have taken comfort that his lot could improve.

Playing on the streets at that time largely devoid of motor cars, it was possible to pick up old bits of bogey roll and thrown away 'dowts'. It wasn't long before Archie MacArthur and Johnny thought they would try putting them in their mouths as older boys did and lighting them. On the day Archie in fun pushed him off a wall, Johnny inhaled his first cigarette and started a lifelong habit. He was eight.

Oban was a small but thriving town in 1920. Kelly's Directory of Scotland claims a population of 6344 with Alexander MacArthur as Provost and Patrick Cooper as town crier. Joseph Perpoli practised dentistry in Kimberley House and groceries were supplied to the townsfolk by Thomas Taylor and Philip Queree. His wife found everlasting fame in the local version of the children's street song

'1,2,3 O'Leery,
I saw Lily Queree
Sitting on her bumbaleeree,
Eating chocolate babies.'

Maxton and White had a fruiterer's business at 86 George Street and the Buttercup Dairy Company sold provisions at Columba Buildings. Henry Scrivens captured for posterity moments grand and ordinary with his camera and Sinclair and Paterson supplied all that mattered in stationery. Boats were built by Donald MacDonald at Cardingmill, Anderson and Nisbet fulfilled many of the plumbing demands of the growing town from their premises at 32 Combie Street while Black and Skinner and Chalmers' Warehouse clothed the population in tartan, tweed or taffeta according to inclination.

In the 1920's, as he grew from boy to man, friendships were made which would last a lifetime, some with people whose names he didn't know. Many of his generation of Obanachs were known by nickname only. Johnny's was John the Lawyer.

With parents and granny now dead, he moved to Mossfield Drive to share a home with his sister and her new husband, Alastair MacRae. Work was difficult to come by so any opportunity of employment was welcome. One of his most enjoyable jobs was that of gardener to Dr. Guy at Eadar Glinn, where the young Johnny became knowledgeable about and captivated by the natural world.

He eventually found a permanent post as trainee grocer and also worked part-time for Chalmer's Warehouse as a delivery boy. Between the two he managed to earn enough to support himself and give his sister something towards his keep. He would say many years afterwards that nothing could ever repay her for what she had given him—a home when he had none, a family to be part of and, above all, love.

Recreation and sport played an important part in the lives of the young of the town in the 20's and 30's. As in the rest of the world, economic depression resulted in day to day uncertainty and an escape could often be found in the various activities on offer. The Band of Hope held weekly meetings in the Congregational Church Hall and these were always well attended. Mr. Dugald Campbell (F.R.G.S.) gave Limelight Lectures, recounting 'thrilling experiences in Central Africa' or, if you were of a musical persuasion, the Kinderspiel Operatic Junior Musical Association was the place to be.

Like other boys of his age, Johnny loved football and shared his loyalties between Drimvargie Swifts and Combie United. Badminton was a favourite winter pastime, partly because of the attraction of mixed doubles and partly because he could represent the Argylls in the Oban Badminton League. He was very fit and agile and enjoyed much success. His stamina and resilience were to serve him well.

Oban Pipe Band was a major influence in his young life. With the encouragement of his brother-in-law, a piper, Johnny learned to play the tenor drum. At that time, there was need for only one more drummer in the band so a coin had to be tossed between the two contenders. Unfortunately for Peter MacCulloch, Johnny won the toss and took his place in the back row. The Band became one of the enduring loves of his life.

Perhaps the greatest influence in his life as a boy, as with many other young men from similar backgrounds, was the Territorial Army. As much to escape the constraints that poverty and the mundanity of everyday life placed on him, he joined the T.A.—$8^{th}$ Argyll and Sutherland Highlanders—when he was eighteen, and attended his first camp at Machrihanish in 1925. Newly kitted out in his uniform and not having much 'tòn' to support his kilt, several large safety pins were used to attach it to his shirt.

Everything was going well until he started to run. The safety pins held but the shirt didn't. It parted company with the kilt, which then descended in folds around his ankles. Fortunately his shirt-tails covered his embarrassment.

Johnny attended many camps and learned many skills in the T.A. including marksmanship and signalling and was promoted to sergeant in August 1939. When he re-engaged for four years in February 1937, he wasn't to know that these and other arts of war were soon to be deployed for real.

# Chapter 18

# Broom Handles and Bad Potatoes.

It wasn't easy being soldier 2974250 when the only gun you had was a broom handle.

Although the official announcement signalling the start of war didn't come until 3rd September, the Territorial Army throughout the country was mobilised on Friday 1st.

When the message 'Clive' was received, the reservists knew that weekend soldiering was over. They were to go to war ahead of the first conscripts. Most of them were older men. Johnny was 33.

Because of the scattered geography of Argyll, it was unusual for more than twenty men to parade in one place, except in the towns. They were not prepared for war. Some didn't have uniforms and others had never used real weapons. What they lacked in hardware, however, they made up for in enthusiasm and the sergeant instructors found it difficult to keep up the pace of training required.

The Battalion numbers doubled in the summer of 1939 and was split to form the 8th and the 11th, which was then based in Cowal with the 8th in Oban. They were men from all walks of civilian life, mustered under the flag. Many of the 8th came from the islands but could not be mobilised until Monday. The M.V. Lochinvar would not break the Sabbath, regardless of events in Europe.

'C' Company assembled in the Drill Hall, Drimvargie Terrace on Friday but were sent home for the weekend until the full contingent of 76 Muileachs and other islanders could join them. They marched from the Drill Hall to the station, boarded the train for Whistlefield and arrived at the West of Scotland Convalescent Home in Dunoon by army truck.

By Monday 4th September, the four companies of Argylls—'A'

from Mid Argyll and Islay, 'B'from Kintyre, 'C' from Oban, Ballachulish and the islands and 'D' from Cowal—had arrived at Dunoon. They numbered over 1000 men. The rest of the month was spent in Cowal learning the arts of war. In four short weeks, Johnny and his comrades were route marched, drilled and trained in the use of weapons.

They were instructed in anti-gas precautions and some became mortar men, some carrier drivers. Johnny specialised in signalling using semaphore flags. A great deal of time was spent on the rifle-range as little opportunity had previously existed to achieve a high standard in marksmanship. Some trained in grey flannels or blue suits with tweed caps or felt hats. Others wore their kilt and service jacket and used their khaki apron while training.

Every battalion had to have its complement of carpenters, clerks, cooks and cobblers and these were trained and allocated from the ranks. During the month at Dunoon, the Battalion was pruned to its fighting size of around 830 men, with the balance joining the 11th.

Only two officers were regular soldiers—Adjutant Captain A. Campbell and Quartermaster H.G Campbell—and they were responsible for ensuring officers and men alike were well versed in army routine. Methodology and instructions, which had evolved over a hundred years, had to be mastered in days. Lack of understanding could cost lives.

The spirit and tradition of a Highland Battalion is embraced in its Pipe Band and, under Pipe Major Nicol MacCallum, the band of the 8th Argylls provided a symbol of unity and pride which was to play a vital role in the months to come. Reveille and Retreat were played morning and night and gradually the assortment of foresters, fishermen, farmers and the rest were moulded into a fighting unit.

On 30th September, orders were received to move to Aldershot where the 51st Highland Division was being marshalled. Under Brigadier Stanley-Clarke, 154 Brigade was made up of the 7th and 8th Battalion Argylls and 6th Black Watch. 152 and 153 Brigades completed the Division. Johnny and his comrades were given three days' leave.

It was probably only then that the reality of the situation hit home. Up until that point, they had been amongst their own, training as they had often done with boys from Argyll. Now, they were getting ready to sail for France.

The ferry took them from Dunoon to Gourock on October 5th,

and from there they travelled in two trains to Maida Barracks in Aldershot. There, what would be two years' training for a regular soldier had to be undertaken in three months. Section, platoon and company training followed, as did field engineering, camouflage, map reading and communications.

By November, every soldier had a uniform consisting of battledress which for practical purposes had replaced the kilt, a Lee Enfield rifle with bayonet and a no. 36 Mills grenade. Each section had a Bren light machine gun and each platoon a .55 Boyes anti-tank rifle and a 2- inch mortar. However, no ammunition was available for either the rifle or the mortar until the middle of January 1940 and high explosive bombs were only issued after France had fallen. The Battalion had at its disposal four 15cwt trucks with mountings for anti-aircraft defence Bren guns. 3-inch mortars were carried on similar vehicles.

New weapons and the paraphernalia of war began to filter through and the Battalion was further pruned and later augmented with Royal Scots Fusiliers and regular soldiers from the Lowlands. By the end of November, Battalion and Brigade exercises were being undertaken. On 12th December, the Battalion marched to its new quarters at Quebec Barracks, Bordon and there, training continued until Christmas.

'C' Company was now under the command of Captain John Inglis, the Battalion led by Lt.-Col. Hamish Grant with Major Lorne Campbell second-in-command.

Immediately after Christmas, the whole Division was given ten days' leave. Boarding the train to take them south again after New Year, Johnny and his fellow soldiers felt a mixture of fear, excitement and apprehension and wondered when they would again look out over Oban Bay. For some, it would be more than five years. Many would never see Argyll again.

On 2nd February, the Battalion left Bordon in two trains for Southampton, embarked on the S.S. Vienna and sailed for France at nightfall. Arriving in Le Havre, they were eventually transported by train to the first billet near Bolbec. The final few miles were covered on foot in the dark. The weather was at its worst—sleet and snow hampering their movements. They were wearing greatcoats and carrying full packs and weapons as well as one blanket, which added to their struggle. In addition, the local guides were unsure of the correct route to take and this too hindered progress. 'A' and 'C'

Companies were housed in barns and sheds in Melamare, with few provisions available due to the non-arrival of their stores. The thaw came at last but turned the ground into mud and brought fog and rain. Then the frost returned, making ruts and ridges of the earth and the terrain largely impassable.

Daily, orders were posted that 'Breakfast will be consumed at 0700 hrs and a haversack ration will be issued to all ranks. Picks and shovels will be taken for digging latrines and scrubbing materials for cleaning billets.'

On February 11$^{th}$, orders came that the Battalion was to move. Johnny, like the rest, was loaded into a railway cattle truck, marked with the legend 'hommes 40, chevaux 8'. Despite a layer of straw on the floors, the overnight journey was long and cold. The one crumb of comfort came from the engine driver who obliged some of the men with boiling water through a blackened hose connected to the boiler. He would direct a jet of steaming water into their dixies which already contained dry tea. Johnny was already learning to make the most of a difficult situation should any opportunity arise and to find kindness in the actions of ordinary people.

They arrived the following morning in Sainghin-en-Weppes near Lille and were relieved to find the advance party had secured better billets for them. Many were in schools, lofts or empty rooms in houses. Nearly all had electric light. Unlike their previous hosts, the people of Sainghin were very friendly and welcoming, many remembering the courage and friendship of Highlanders from another war.

Because of the proximity to Lille, the men were occasionally granted passes to visit the town where they enjoyed the physical and 'spiritual' hospitality of the locals.

Sometimes the temptation to sample more French spirit than was good for them would result in passing out parades more commonly seen outside The Star Inn than Sandhurst.

The British Expeditionary Force by this time had been in France for three or four months without any contact with the enemy. During this time, small British formations were attached to the French Army for up to fifteen days. Here in the Saar, German patrols were constantly on the move and provided the first time experience for many of being shot at in anger. This arrangement acclimatised many of the new battalions to battle.

At the end of March, they moved twenty-five miles to the north.

Here, 154 Brigade was given the job of digging a section of anti-tank ditch to supposedly reinforce the lines of defence already in place. Seeing this as a more practical alternative to training, the Highlanders worked laboriously at the task, supervised by members of the intelligence section of the Battalion, who had honed their excavation skills at the Benmore Forestry School outside Dunoon. 16th April saw them move to Metz, near the Maginot Line, then to Kedange. There were four lines of defence of the Maginot Line. The most forward line—Ligne de Contact—was an outpost line. Behind that, the Ligne de Soutien, Ligne de Recueil and Ligne d'Arret were lines of support.

The 51st was positioned near Hombourg-Budange lying in the rich, fertile land of Lorraine between the Saar and Moselle. The green, rolling countryside contrasted markedly with their previous positions. Spring was in the air and Johnny smelled the sweet smell of Lily of the Valley and apple blossom. War seemed comfortably distant.

On April 27th, the Battalion was ordered to relieve the 7th on the Ligne de Soutien.

They marched forward at night, with rifles loaded as a precaution against German patrols and this was the first time Johnny realised that shooting at real Germans was an imminent possibility. Battalion H.Q. was set up at Waldweistroff. During the day, the Company were kept busy improving defences and wiring and at night they took their turn at sentry duty. Sleep was fitful and often forfeited, resulting in an inevitable loss of alertness and efficiency.

By the beginning of May, the Battalion moved up to the front line with 'C' Company based at Grindorff and night attacks became increasingly more intense.

Those on duty at night were very tense and edgy, so much so that the slightest noise, twig breaking, bird or animal sound was regarded as suspicious. After six days, they were relieved by the Black Watch and the men looked forward to a few days and nights of relative rest.

It was not for Johnny or the rest of the B.E.F to question strategies of war. They were trained to obey orders without thinking and to fight to the last if commanded to do so. They went where they were sent, did as they were told and assumed those who gave the orders knew what they were doing. On top of that, the centuries-old tradition of the Highland soldier fighting to the death rather than surrendering was part of their make-up.

They didn't know, and weren't told, that the weaponry and tactics employed by the British and French were woefully inadequate when facing the German war machine.

As late as 1937, repeated attempts had been made by Captain Liddell Hart and Major-General Fuller to convince the military establishment that more importance should be placed on tanks and other armoured vehicles and less on cavalry. By the start of hostilities, only half the necessary lorries had been delivered to the British forces and the French army was still heavily dependent on horse-drawn transport.

Liddell Hart, in particular, as early as 1924, had advocated a change from the trench-based tactics, static and inflexible, which had been employed in the First World War, to an 'expanding torrent' method of attack using armoured forces, concentrated in one place. His own side paid scant regard to his advice but the Germans didn't. The Treaty of Versailles and the punitive measures exacted on the Germans after 1918 meant, in essence, their rearmament programme had started afresh. Where the British and French clung to horse and rifle, the Germans set about modernising their ships, aircraft and weapons and eliminating their obsolete equipment. Where the British and French communicated by flags and even heliographs and relied on dispatch riders to carry commands to the battle front, the Germans coordinated their attacks through the use of radio, enabling officers to be in the front line with their troops. Where the British and French dug ditches and settled into trench positions, the Germans favoured Liddell Hart's ideas of a new philosophy of warfare—blitzkrieg or lightning war. These ideas found widespread support amongst many high-ranking German officers, including the newly appointed commander of 7th Panzer Division, Erwin Rommel.

So it was, therefore, on the 10th May, the German army attacked Belgium and Holland in a coordinated offensive using bombers and paratroopers. So swift was the attack that half the Belgian air force was destroyed on the ground and key bridges were secured before the allies could react.

On 13th May, the Germans launched a major assault on the whole front and the 51st Division was forced to withdraw. As the Germans continued their two-pronged attack, the French, who were in command of the Division, were thrown into disarray. Orders were confused and misunderstood, travel arrangements disorganised. The civilian population fled in thousands, jamming transport routes and hindering movement. Roads were blocked with abandoned vehicles. It was to be almost a week before men and machines were reunited, by which time the Division was cut off from the rest of the B.E.F., which was heading for Dunkirk and evacuation. On 28$^{th}$ May, the 51$^{st}$. reassembled along the River Bresle and on 2$^{nd}$ June, moved to a line from the coast towards Abbeville—a front of fourteen miles—to try to drive back the enemy from the Somme. Headquarters were set up, firstly at Escarbotin then at St. Blimont. On the left, Johnny and the rest of 'C' Company under Captain Inglis were based at Tilloy. The various companies held defensive blocks rather than a continuous line and the land between them could not even be covered by fire.

Some groups were a mile apart. There was no wireless communication forward of Battalion H.Q. Dispatch riders had to deliver all orders and collect all reports. Few of the French officers spoke much English and few of the British officers had much French. The opportunities for mistakes and confusion were plentiful. While the 51$^{st}$ Highland Division was beginning the battle for Abbeville and striving to support the French, seventy miles away the last of the British Expeditionary Force was being shipped back to Britain from Dunkirk to a heroes' welcome, leaving Johnny and his comrades without any support and dangerously vulnerable.

The next three days were comparatively restful. It was hot and dry. Farms that had been abandoned offered a ready supply of milk, cheese and eggs. At night, patrols were sent out to establish enemy positions. At three o'clock on June 4$^{th}$, the artillery of the combined French and British forces opened fire and, half an hour later, tanks and infantry moved forward to their first objective. The job of 154 Brigade, positioned on the left, was to prevent the enemy from reinforcing the bridgehead but it soon became obvious that the Division had no hope of holding the advancing Germans. The front was too long and those given the task of defending it, too few. But nowhere was it abandoned without fighting.

The following day, the Germans launched their offensive against the Somme-Aisne line—Fall Rot (Operation Red) and 'C' Company began moving back to take up position at Belloy. 14$^{th}$ Platoon, under Lt. James Mellor, were nearby at Pende, where they opened fire on a patrol of enemy cavalry at 4.30 in the morning and inflicted heavy losses. One wounded German officer was taken into Platoon Headquarters for identification. Reports were sent, informing that German cavalry were dismounting and using the village as an assembly point. Tanks were also visible.

For over two hours, Captain Inglis had to use field telephone to relay targets and information to the gunners behind. At about 6 o'clock, Colonel Grant arrived and, at the same time, 14 Platoon reported being in great difficulty. Orders were given to shell the village and 14 Platoon was instructed to withdraw from Pende to Tilloy when the opportunity arose. This was achieved with few casualties and they were able to join the rest of their Company. By 9 a.m., the village of St. Blimont was in danger of being surrounded. 'C' Company fought valiantly over the next three hours to hold the village but Brigadier Clarke ordered them to evacuate when it became necessary. They withdrew to the next village- Belloy—where they had to go into action again to cover 'D' Company as they took up their positions.

At about 6 o'clock that evening, Johnny was issued with half a tin of M&V rations—the first meal he had had since the previous evening. There had been no opportunity for even a drink of tea. Hunger, thirst and lack of sleep left him weak and drained of energy.

But there was to be no rest yet.

Around 9.30 p.m., a message was received from Major Young of the 7th Argylls stating that he considered the position untenable and that he was pulling back. Captain Inglis decided to do the same, as he had no news of 'A' and 'B' Companies, he didn't know the whereabouts of the 7th Argylls and no contact had been received from anyone south of Belloy. Furthermore, anti-tank guns and artillery had not been seen since early morning and the location of Battalion H.Q. was unknown. The move back was timed for 2330 hours.

Just as they were moving off, a dispatch rider arrived and told Captain Inglis that 'D' Company was returning and that 'C' and 'D' Company were to hold Belloy and nearby Escarbotin at all costs. The Platoons returned to their positions at the Chateau de Belloy and spent the night there without incident. 14 Platoon were in the grounds, 300 yards away from the chateau. At 7o'clock in the morning, the Germans launched a ferocious attack and the lines had to be shortened.

By ten o'clock, the whole force, now only about 200 men, was within the grounds of the chateau and the number of casualties was rising dramatically. Company H.Q. was moved into the chateau and a first aid post was set up in its drawing room.

The aim of the Battalion at this point was to hold the roads around Belloy and Escarbotin and, although the area around the chateau continued to be a pocket of resistance, they were no longer fulfilling their objective. Meanwhile the rest of the Division was being gradually pulled back with the hope of evacuating the men from Le Havre.

Back at the chateau, the men were becoming extremely weak from lack of food and sleep. All that could be offered them was one tablespoon each of a mixture of turnip and bad potatoes. That was the only food they had that day although an effort was made to find two cows, which had been seen grazing in the fields earlier.

The Battalion pipes had been lost with the rest of the baggage and this proved a great setback. The evocative and stirring sound united and galvanised the men as nothing else could and reminded them of home. Their loss was keenly felt.

Captain Inglis could see that the position was now impossible. The chateau was surrounded and there was no likelihood of reinforcements arriving. Communication from H.Q. had stopped. He decided to hold a conference with his junior officers to discuss their next move. The plan was that some of 'D' Company should try to get out but, despite the imminent danger, to a man they said they would stand by 'C' Company:—Là a' bhlàir 's math na càirdean—. During that afternoon, enemy mortar fire intensified and two attacks were launched on the chateau. Despite their desperately weak state, the remnants of 'C' company fought them off, inflicting heavy casualties on the enemy. Just before dark, six tanks took up position north of the chateau and fire works were set off as a signal that the position was held by the enemy. The night of the 6th June was relatively quiet and nothing moved until 7 a.m. when it became clear that the Germans had brought in reinforcements. The men were issued with one cooked preserved egg and a lump of sugar each, with some getting a mouthful of cocoa.

The Germans surrounding the chateau numbered 1500 infantry, 20 tanks, 10 armoured cars and 2 Field Guns. When the final assault came on the 7th, all the men had been driven into the chateau. By 3o'clock the enemy were in the building and all ammunition had been used up. Now down to 150 men, they had held back the powerful German war machine with rifles and light machine guns. They had nothing left. They were sitting targets. Through Captain Inglis' mind ran thoughts of the waste of lives if they continued fighting. He reluctantly ordered 'cease fire'.

Alasdair Carmichael with 'D' Company described the final minutes.

"All around us now, thicker and closer with every minute, exploding mortar shells came down like rain, tearing great limbs from trees that had, part of the day, afforded us shade from the blistering sun; gouging vast craters in the garden beside us and in front, throwing earth into our eyes and threatening to burst our ears with their awful noise.

Whistles were shrilling now, from closer to the crumbling chateau where dust clouds rose from shell-torn masonry. Then the shelling ceased, cut off with a suddenness that hurt the ears.

The battle was over.

Someone told me it was ten past four."

# Chapter 19

# Behind the Wire

It wasn't easy being P.O.W. number 804 (Arbeitskommando 1401) when you had nothing to wear on your feet and you were always hungry.

As Johnny looked out of the window of his hut at Bleicherode work camp, his mind would often return to the dark days following capture in June 1940. His body had longed for sleep and food but little had been forthcoming. His mind had found the idea of surrender difficult to comprehend but, as the haze of the last few terrible days cleared, he thanked God often that at least he was alive, unlike so many of his comrades.

In the moment of surrender, the German Commander had wanted to know the whereabouts of the rest of the men who had caused his troops such trouble and inflicted such heavy casualties. He looked in disbelief at the few who had held out for so long against such overpowering odds.

Two incidents had occurred immediately after cease-fire which could have resulted in the execution of the prisoners. As a burial party was organised to inter the fourteen dead Argylls from around the chateau, one of the party had produced his remaining grenade and was about to pull the pin and throw it into the German ranks. But for the presence of mind of $2^{nd}$ Lieutenant Bruce Cheape in throwing it into the open grave, Johnny and his friends would have been shot.

The second incident involved a German who had been brought in, apparently with his throat cut. Despite having spent the last few days trying to kill or maim the Highlanders with their powerful arsenal, the Germans hated the use of knives. Fortunately, a German doctor confirmed that the wound had been caused by a bullet. Again, Johnny's life was spared.

Then, for a few, incredible minutes, German and Jock had sat down together on the grassy terrace in front of the smouldering chateau and exchanged water bottles. Some Germans offered their prisoners bread and sausage. It was a moving moment of goodwill in a brutal day. All the uninjured men were marched to a field near Abbeville where they wearily lay down on the grass and succumbed to fitful sleep. Meanwhile, the remainder of the 51$^{st}$ Highland Division had been pulled back to St.Valery-en-Caux with the hope of evacuation. When it became clear that the few ships, which had arrived to bring them home, could not reach land, the situation had become impossible. The cliffs along the coast at St Valery are 300 feet high and anyone moving on the beach was an easy target for the gunners now positioned on the top. The Germans under Rommel had virtually surrounded the town and ammunition was all but used up.

Despite that, when Major Hill of the 4$^{th}$ Battalion Cameron Highlanders assembled his men and, with tears running down his cheeks, told them to 'ground arms', the men could not comprehend what he was ordering them to do. To a man, they held fast to their rifles. It was only when the order was repeated and it became apparent that the whole town would be sacked and every one in it killed did they, reluctantly, obey.

The other half of the 8$^{th}$ Battalion, 'A' and 'B' Companies, had managed to evade capture and reached Le Havre and home, unaware that the men of 'C' and 'D' Companies were now prisoners of war.

For Johnny and over 10,000 other British soldiers, the long walk to captivity began from the field at Abbeville. French and Senegalese tripled the numbers. The long line of struggling, demoralised prisoners, guarded on both sides by armed soldiers, covered about 20 miles a day through the baking heat of a French summer. Uppermost in their minds were the memories of their fallen comrades and the humiliation of defeat. Wracked with the continual pain of hunger and swollen, blistered feet, throats and lips parched and utterly exhausted from weeks with little sleep, the dispirited remnants of the proud Highland Division moved north.

Past Amiens and Arras, by St Pol and Sainghin and Seclin, through the land around Lille and Tournai the column moved, each day bringing renewed hope of finding food or help from local people; most nights bringing disappointment. Evenings would find the men camped in a barbed-wire enclosure using their helmets as pillows and greatcoats as blankets. The heat of the day was hard to bear but the cold at night was worse and those who had jettisoned their greatcoats were forced to sleep on the bare ground with no cover.

Food was intermittent and sparse. The first three days of marching had seen the two-mile long column crossing crop fields and meadows and the only food was what could be foraged along the way. Raw potatoes, apples, cherries and pears, not yet ripe, were eaten in the absence of anything else. Severe stomach cramps and diarrhoea followed, further weakening the men. It was to be a full week before Johnny had anything resembling a meal and even then it was a thin slice of rye bread and one tin of M and V rations between two. Where local women offered food and water, they were frequently and brutally beaten back. Pots of soup by the roadside were, more often than not, kicked over by some of the more sadistic guards. Battalion rations and NAAFI supplies, which had been looted by the French Army were, unbelievably and cruelly, offered for sale to the starving men at inflated prices along the march. On through Belgium, Johnny and his comrades wearily struggled, thick clouds of dust billowing up from the road, choking their already parched and swollen throats.

Water bottles were filled in the morning and could only be supplemented by rainwater running off roofs following a shower of rain. To the thirsty men, nothing was more precious or tasted as sweet as that newly fallen rain.

Some relief came when the column reached Flanders, where the Red Cross gave out food and registered the prisoners' names. At least word could now get home that Johnny was alive.

As feet blistered, festered and gave out, many fell down exhausted and gave up. If the crack of a rifle butt on the head or the point of a bayonet in the back didn't get them to their feet, they were left to be loaded on a truck later—or just left.

The thought of escape occupied minds on the long march. Many made attempts to break free from the long, weary line only to be recaptured through bad luck or treachery. Others succeeded in evading capture and getting home. One such incident involved three Ballachulish men who made their way back to Scotland by speaking only in Gaelic when stopped by the Germans. Their achievement in outwitting the enemy earned them each a Military

Medal but the humiliation felt by the German intelligence service was not be forgotten or forgiven readily.

On past Renaix, Aalst, Ghent, Lokeren and Antwerp they tramped, growing weaker and more dejected. Eventually the column of prisoners arrived at Hulst in Holland where the River Rhine empties into the North Sea. They had covered almost 300 miles.

If the past three weeks on foot had been exhausting, the next four days and five nights were unspeakably brutal. Johnny was near the front of the line and was loaded on to the first of eight barges. As many men as possible were packed on the deck and the rest were loaded into the hold. Then the hatches were battened down. Each man had only his own length and breadth to move. There was little air and the heat was unbearable. When it became obvious that the majority of the prisoners could not survive these conditions, the hatches were opened and they were allowed to climb on deck for a brief breath of air. Toilet was performed from planks overhanging the river.

By this time, Johnny was almost delirious with hunger. For some reason, those on the first barge did not get the standard black loaf given to the others. The barges had previously been used to carry coal and before that, cereal crops, so the starving men were reduced to scraping in corners for blackened grains of wheat to keep themselves alive. Roddy MacPherson, a Seaforth from Glenelg, remembers tying belts and braces to his helmet to fish filthy water from the Rhine—their only source of water. A guard sat on deck with a machine gun permanently trained on them.

Amongst the prisoners was a number of French who had capitulated in great numbers. They had haversacks filled with bread or water or wine. In desperation, Roddy begged one of them for a sip of water. The Frenchman threw back his head and laughed.

"If you want water, lie on your back, open your mouth and wait for rain!"

The normally gentle Roddy snapped and leapt at the Frenchman, knocking him to the ground. Then a rifle butt felled him. The rest of the prisoners, exhausted and starving though they were, circled the guard and threatened to throw him overboard. The incident was eventually defused and thereafter, the guard treated the men more sympathetically. By the time they were taken off the barges, the men were covered in sores and their clothes crawling with lice, which they tried to burn off with lighted papers. Many had eggs hatch under their skin. Some had dysentery and all suffered from stomach cramps and diarrhoea.

They arrived at Emmerich in Germany on $2^{nd}$ July and were marched at night for three miles to a temporary encampment set up just outside the town. Johnny, like the rest, was issued with bread and margarine and had his photo taken to be used as propaganda. There he remained for six days, living off coffee, soup and occasionally cheese or treacle—a banquet after the privation of the past few weeks.

However, despite being rested and fed, his ordeal was far from over. Workers were needed for the mines in Poland and were selected from the ranks of prisoners. Men who had trained together, fought together and suffered together were separated and transported in different directions. Loaded into cattle trucks with a black loaf, some water and a bucket for a toilet for forty men, Johnny moved on again. Many were transported to Torun in Poland to work in the mines. Johnny and the rest headed for boggy ground near Bad Sulza and Stalag 1X C in northern Germany where temporary camps had been set up. Already, the men were again filthy, starving and exhausted. From here, detachments of prisoners were sent to the ten or twelve satellite arbeitskommandos or work camps.

Weary, dispirited and a long way from his beloved Argyll, Johnny's heart soared when, on entering a windowless room, he heard the words "Ciamar a tha thu ?"

Without thinking he replied in Gaelic and was immediately put to one side. The embarrassment the Germans had felt at being hoodwinked by escapees speaking in Gaelic had made them resolve never to be humiliated in such a way again. All Gaelic speakers were to be separated and sent to a special work camp. Rudolstadt seemed a pleasant enough town at first sight but there, Johnny and fifty or so other Gaelic speakers, some Welshmen, two Irishmen and a number of Free Masons were segregated. Housed in a small room, the men lived without water and a 40-gallon drum in the middle of the floor sufficed as a toilet. They walked four miles to a sand quarry under guard, worked a twelve-hour shift till 6p.m. and walked four miles back. They couldn't wash or shave and were fed on ersatz coffee made from burnt barley, one slice of black bread and one bowl of watery carrot soup each day. Walking to the quarry and back, there was always the slim chance of finding a crust a dog had missed or picking up a jettisoned cigarette end. For over a month, Johnny and the others were made to pay for a crime they had no knowledge of and no hand in.

From Rudolstadt, Johnny was sent, briefly, to Unterbreizbach to work in the salt mines. He was then transferred to Bleicherode.

Arbeitskommando 1401 at Bleicherode seemed like heaven after Rudolstadt and Unterbreizbach. Here, Johnny was reunited with many of his comrades and housed in a more conventional prison camp. Yes, there were guards with dogs and barbed wire but he now had a whole loaf to himself—to last a week. Here, he had ersatz coffee morning and night and here, he had soup made from potatoes, which was slightly more palatable and nutritious than at Rudolstadt.

Bleicherode today is a small village, nestling at the foot of the Hartz Mountains.

Its main industry is the large Kaliwerk or potash mine a short distance from the railway station. In 1940, it looked much the same but with a branch line taking trains into the heart of the mine. Here, Johnny was to spend four and a half years of his life. The camp was within the perimeter fence of the mine. Long huts, with three, twelve-bedded rooms in each, slept up to two hundred men, with straw sacks for beds. Seven feet high pipes, partially filled with slag from the mines, were scattered throughout the compound. These the Germans used as air-raid shelters for themselves. The prisoners had to take their chances in the open.

Work in the mine was long and hard, with the men working almost 9 hours daily. Few of the Highlanders had ever worked below ground and they found adapting to this difficult. Ill-health was, of course, common place and many suffered boils and salt rashes.

Johnny's health deteriorated and salt poisoned his system so badly that he was taken to the military hospital at Obermassfeld to be treated. He remained there for some time before he was transferred back to camp. Despite these adverse conditions, Johnny was able to find the beauty in nature that had always uplifted him. One day in September 1941, while deep down in the mine, he unearthed an exquisite, mother-of-pearl shell, a legacy from another age. He treasured this find and in years to come, would look on it as a reminder of how beautiful life can be even in desperate circumstances.

The men had two Sundays off a month and were paid camp money for their labours. This money was marked with a triangle and could only be spent within Bleicherode at an inflated rate and in certain shops. They were often entitled to backdated pay and, when enough money was accrued, groups would be allowed to go into town under guard, to purchase a variety of musical instruments or sports equipment to supplement those sent by the Red Cross. Johnny was given a mandolin. Others had guitars, accordions, banjos and a good selection of brass instruments. Eventually, a set of pipes was acquired. Out of this, emerged bands and orchestras, which lifted the spirit of players and audience. In fact, taking up the front row of most concerts were the German officers and guards, some of whom came from musical backgrounds and appreciated the effort involved in practising and performing music.

Those working night shift were able to attend funerals of comrades that had succumbed to illness or disease and were amazed at the dignity with which their captors treated the dead. Elaborate wreaths were provided, many bearing a swastika—regarded by the Germans as a mark of high honour—and full military honours accompanied the burial in the civilian cemetery.

Every evening, the whole camp would be lined up and counted. It would often take four or five attempts to get the numbers right as much shuffling and discreet changing of position ensured confusion. As Archie Gillespie recalled, those on bakery duty would also use every trick to distract the guard so that, without fail, the number of loaves arriving in camp was always more than had been allocated. Every opportunity was taken to confound the guards and cause maximum disruption.

Communal tasks were allocated according to previous experience. As well as working in the mine, some men like Johnnie Simpson and Alasdair MacNeill from Mull became boot repairers, vital when the only footwear available were the army issue boots worn when captured. If boots were lost or irreparable, feet were wrapped in rags and wooden clogs were worn—summer and winter. Some were given work as builders, others in forestry and gardening. A few men were sent to build roads for new houses being constructed. To alleviate the mind-numbing and morale-sapping boredom that was beginning to affect the men, permission was given for a sports-field to be created out of a disused quarry across the road from the camp. One of the prisoners, Harry

MacAulay, was a surveyor so his skills were employed to start the project. There followed many weeks of hard digging, levelling and raking the cinder surface till it looked like a satisfactory sports pitch. The men were elated and talk turned to football, shinty, boxing and athletics, all of which were encouraged by the guards.

The Germans, many of whom were also far from home, enjoyed the matches almost as much as the prisoners and even encouraged local children to learn new skills from the men. Teams from other camps were invited and tournaments set up. The men always knew when Dennis 'Tiger' MacNeill was in goal. Whether through excitement or terror of letting in a goal, he would roar like a tiger if the ball headed his way. The pitch was outside the barbed wire of the camp and being able to leave the compound gave a great boost to faltering spirits.

During the winter, Johnny joined Dennis, Roddy MacPherson and Freddie MacAllister in a work-party to thin beech trees in a nearby wood. Care had to be taken to select branches with straight shafts and the right amount of bend. These were destined to be shaped into camans by Gregor McBain from Kingussie. Finding a ball, however, was more difficult. A cork was obtained and methodically, all old jumpers were appropriated and unravelled. Carefully, the wool was wound round the cork, backwards and forwards, until it met with the approval of the man from Badenoch.

By this time, Red Cross parcels were beginning to filter through to the camps and the arrival of extra food, a packet of cigarettes, a bar of chocolate and especially socks improved the quality of life for the men immeasurably. Looting was inevitable and, from time to time, the prisoners would complain that their parcels from home had been tampered with. Roddy had been told that a parcel had arrived for him.

He knew his cousin in Glenelg had promised to send him a jumper and, when it became apparent that his parcel had gone missing, the guards were questioned.

The Germans hated dishonesty and punishment for theft was a transfer to the Russian front. This was tantamount to a death sentence for the guards. There was one less guard on duty the following day. He was found with a bullet through his mouth a short time later. He had used the water barrel to muffle the sound of his final shot.

Nothing from the outside world could be wasted. Every man in the camp was exhorted to keep all the string from his parcels and on no account was it to be cut.

Painstakingly, all the lengths were knotted and looped into a net to complete the shinty and football goals. All cleaning and laundry had to be done by the men in between work and sleep. A wooden table was set up on the cobbles in the enclosure and there, shirts, underwear and uniforms were soaped and scrubbed. Water was filled from an adjacent trough and brought in pails and basins to rinse the washing. Clothes dried in the sun or were worn damp, depending on the weather and the time of year.

Spuds and vegetables were peeled and prepared in the trough by those detailed to be cooks. Duty rosters were drawn up to cover other communal tasks. The latrines were housed in a hut between the sleeping units next to the sick bay. Toilet for two hundred men was performed through holes in the wooden planking and a pipe drained the effluent into a tank at the far end of the hut. Those on latrine duty had the odious task of emptying the tank and disposing of its contents. On one occasion, when Roddy was on duty, he was overcome by a moment of despair and homesickness. He calmly went over to the stinking, fetid, decomposing excrement. In his cupped hands he lifted the sewage to his face and said to the guards,

"I will gladly drink this if you will only let me go home. Please let me go home"—

As the years of war slowly dragged on, the men became ever resourceful in finding ways to make their captivity bearable and to alleviate boredom.

Graham Hopper was known as 'der professor' and, with his spectacles and shining, domed head, looked very much like the statistician he was in civilian life. He was concerned that, as months of captivity became years, the spirit of the men would be ground down. He decided to set about starting a theatre company in the camp and enlisted the help of Alasdair Carmichael—'the bishop'—as playwright.

Christmas 1942 saw the premiere of Babes in the Wood—a pantomime. Courtiers, princes and princesses, wandering minstrels, wicked stepmother and fairy godmother shared the stage with the 'Babes', Jeannie and Wullie. John the Lawyer played Third Huntsman and, if the reviews on his treasured programme are to be believed, he acted his role well. The preparations gave the men a new impetus and enthusiasm. Sets had to be designed and built;

clothing purloined and adapted to make costumes; carpenters, electricians and painters had to beg, borrow, steal or invent ways of achieving their objectives; scripts written, chorus and orchestra assembled and rehearsed, make-up made up and applied, scenery planned and painted, programmes designed and printed. The effort involved in producing the show acted as a great unifier.

New friendships, which would last beyond war, were formed—comrades in arms and comrades in captivity.

The pain felt by many at being far from home, especially at Christmas was, in some way, alleviated by pantomimes and concerts. Guards and guarded would unite in carol singing, both with their own thoughts of family and home and Johnny's hymn book, snow-stained at Stille Nacht, was to evoke bitter-sweet memories in the years to come.

New Year was traditionally a more important festival in the Highlands and being a prisoner in Germany could not be allowed to spoil that. With eager anticipation, the teuchters waited for the 'bells'. For months, they had taken it in turn to secretly fish potatoes out of the store using a nail on a stick. An engineer with some basic knowledge of chemistry was coerced into putting his skills to use. He extracted enough alcohol from meths to make a base for the brew. Raisins, potatoes, boot polish and anything that could be found was added to the preparation by a couple of Islay lads who could be expected to know a thing or two about distilling. It would be a Hogmanay to remember!

Unfortunately, when they buried their uisge beatha between two huts, the ground was soft and easily turned over. When they came to dig it up in time for New Year, frost had rendered exhumation impossible. The ground was frozen solid. Celebrations and reputations were distinctly diminished that year. The Ne'erday shinty match, however, was played and the celebrating, in any small way, of the customs and traditions of the Highlands kept spirits up even if release seemed a long way off. With the reappearance of the pipes and a measure of home comforts, Bleicherode camp was better than some and Johnny grew accustomed to waiting out the war in this pleasant corner of Germany. The camp commandant was eager to photograph the men if it provided an opportunity for propaganda. Official camp photos would be sent home, showing how well the men were being looked after and what the Germans were doing for them. It was illegal to photograph anything without an official stamp. Ingenuity was called for. The ubiquitous potato again came into its own. A slice was taken and a newly stamped photo was urgently acquired. The potato was placed on the stamp, the resulting image transferred to paper and the process repeated to render the stamp the right way round. Many illegal and informal snaps were taken this way and avoided detection. Had they been discovered, their architects could have been shot.

As the years dragged on, the guards and prisoners became, if not friends, at least understanding of one another. Regulations were more relaxed and guards, on pain of being shot if one escaped, were allowed to sign out prisoners on a Sunday, to help them in their own gardens and homes. Johnny was able to meet civilians for the first time in many years and came to have an understanding of and respect for many who made his ordeal bearable. There were many happy times to counter the sad.

The overriding thoughts in most minds were of home and family. Johnny would compose poems to ease the longing and, though these would not find a home amongst the great literature of our time, were written with genuine emotion and real pathos. They summed up what most in the camp felt. His thoughts would always turn to his beloved Oban, a town whose history mirrored his own family's.

Oban is, by anyone's measure, an attractive town. It is cradled in a setting of natural beauty that surely ranks amongst the most captivating anywhere on earth. To climb Ardconnel Hill on a June evening to watch the sun set behind the Table of Lorn, throwing up searchlights of every colour into the blueing sky and setting alight the clouds with blazing brilliance, must surely move the most impassive of hearts;—or to stand on Pulpit Hill and watch the comings and goings of the ferries and small boats before eyes are drawn beyond the bay to Dunollie Castle and the enchantment of islands that lie scattered across the Firth of Lorn to Mull and Morvern;—or to wander along the Ganavan Road on a spring evening, heavy scented with wild hyacinths, drinking in the beauty of the place and reawakening deep-held memories of the folk who laboured there in another time.

*An t'ob* means the bay, harbour or shallow pool. Add to that the Gaelic diminutive ending *an,* and you have the naming of the place—the wee bay or harbour. It was home to Johnny and at least four generations of his family before him. And he loved the place more than he could say.

Growing from a scattering of fishermen's dwellings built where *Loch-a-mhuillin* emptied into the sea and drawing in long established clachans in Gleann Cruitten and Gleann Seilach, Oban had expanded and developed into the bustling, friendly, prosperous town it was in 1939. It was studded with gems, some natural others reminders of a previous age.

Before the railway came to the town in 1880, the sea washed up on the gentle-sloping beach below Shore Street. Here, the local fishermen would haul their boats far enough up the shore to be safe even at high tide. The row of whitewashed cottages along Shore Street was home to these fishermen and, by 1763, along with the small townships around Loch-a-Mhuillin, formed the beginnings of the present town.

It was not only evoking the beauty and peace of the town that brought him comfort. Memories and snapshots of his life there and the kindness of the people would find him often weeping into his pillow. He would think on the black night when the MacBrayne's steamer, 'The Grenadier' caught fire sometime after midnight while moored at the pier. The Captain Archibald MacArthur and two of his crew, including the young cabin boy, were burnt to death. He remembered the frantic efforts of the locals to save them and of hearing the desperate pleas from the crew, unable to get out of the port-holes, for someone to shoot them before the fire reached them.

He would think on the tragedy of two young lads, lads he had been in school with, who had decided to go skating on the Distillery Pond near the tower. They had an hour for their dinner break from their jobs with Robertson the Chemist and enjoyed getting out to play for a while. When the first boy fell through the ice, the mother of the older lad saw the accident from her window and frantically called for her son to get off. He refused and went to the aid of his friend. The mother ran to the nearby sanitorium gate and called for help from some workmen. One brought a rope but fell through the ice himself. Only with great difficulty was he hauled out. Dr. Campbell arrived but not in time to save the two youngsters.

The whole of Oban had come to a standstill on the day of the funeral. Shops and businesses closed, window blinds were drawn and the bells of the local churches tolled their sorrow. Scouts and members of The Boys' Brigade lined the road below Heatherbank, home to one of the lads and the coffins, arrayed with cap, belt and haversack, were borne on the shoulders of their fellow Brigade members. As the funeral procession made its way up the Bealach an Righ, the pipe band led the mourners—family, neighbours and people representing all sections of the community. And a piper played The Flowers o' the Forest.

He would think on the Cathedral of Trees at Glencruitten, and the winding road to Cockle Shore, and the old drove road at Kerrera Ferry and the many other delights of the place. It cheered his heart thinking on the wee town by the sea and of the good people who lived there. He vowed he would never leave it if he ever made it home—and he very rarely did.

In the years after the war, Johnny, like many of his comrades, would speak reluctantly and only occasionally of what he had been through and the experiences he had suffered. He would remember the Englishman with a hole in both cheeks where a bullet had entered one and exited the other. He would recall Jackie MacRae from Lochcarron who, one summer, stretched up from his seat on the back of a truck to pick a ripe plum from an overhanging branch, only to fall backwards and break his neck. He would laugh gently when he remembered the time two anxious parents, working in a nearby allotment, constantly checked on their young child who appeared to cry when they were at the bottom of the field but was always asleep when they came to comfort it. They never did discover that Tommy MacMillan could imitate a baby's cry with uncanny accuracy and used his talent to the great annoyance of the Germans. Most of all, he remembered his comrades, men like himself, who had been wrenched from their ordinary lives and sent to hell.

As the summer of 1944 waned, events on the Western front were signalling a change in fortune for the allies. The German guards in Bleicherode became more tolerant and eventually allowed the men permission to go beyond the camp perimeter to swim in a pool in the river. Safe in the knowledge that it could never be disproved, one of the prisoners had regularly boasted his prowess at swimming.

Before the war, he had been a champion. Before the war, he could out-swim practically anyone. Before the war, he had been an ace diver. On the first outing to the pool he was put to the test. He dived spectacularly from the plank and executed a clean entry into the water. He failed to take account of the water only being a few feet deep, however, and it was only when his legs began to flail about and he showed no sign of surfacing that his pals set about pulling him out. His head and arms were well and truly stuck in the sand and it took some time to free him. His life was saved but his reputation as a swimmer was somewhat diminished.

Ajax was an Alsatian belonging to one of the guards. He had his wires crossed at some point in his training because, despite numerous corrective lessons, he was happier in the company of the prisoners than on duty as a guard dog. He joyfully accompanied the men to the river but invariably ended up being rescued. Ajax couldn't swim. Again, resourcefulness was called for. Here was an ally that needed help. Ajax was collared, measured and fitted with water wings to allow him the delight of playing in the river with the men—a small gesture to a dumb animal maybe, but a compassionate deed in a time of adversity, nonetheless.

As March turned to April in 1945, it became clear that the tide had turned and Germany was losing the war. Guards and their officers became nervous and agitated. Increasingly, gunfire could be heard to the west and the nearby town of Nordhausen, home of the V1 and V2 vengeance weapons factory, was being bombed nightly. The men in camp 1401 were caught between fear from danger of friendly fire and desperation to be liberated.

The Germans were becoming anxious and doing all in their power to clear all the camps in the area. The first few days of April became a blur. Chaos and confusion accompanied the men as they were hustled along the road from Bleicherode. As the allies advanced, so the Germans retreated until, one day, Johnny realised the guards had disappeared.

For the first time in five years, he walked the road a free man. He was 39, weighed less than six stone and carried only what he was able to cram into his kit bag.

Far away, from an abandoned radio came, unbelievably, unmistakably, the haunting strains of The Eriskay Love Lilt, filling the air with the sound of home. Over the hill behind him he thought he heard a familiar but long-forgotten sound. Turning, he saw the Stars and Stripes fluttering on a radio antenna. The first tank belonging to the 174th Battalion of U.S. Artillery came over the rise.

Johnny's war was over.

## Chapter 20

## 'With Ears Like Yours'

I would be lying if I said I mind exactly what I was doing the day war was declared. Most likely, working as usual. Poland and the goings on there were of no immediate concern to me and I hoped, like everyone else, that it would all be over soon. The only difference I was aware of was the increased military activity in the area around Crieff.

By the time I had moved there to work, it was commonplace to see lorry loads of soldiers passing through the town and along the network of quiet, country lanes that webbed the area. And it was just my luck for one such lorry to be passing the Post Office at the very minute my knicker elastic perished beyond redemption and my bloomers went into free fall and landed on the pavement. Face flushed, I could only barely make out the stooshie and ribald heckling as I nonchalantly bent down and pocketed the redundant breeks.

I spent the next two years working at Auld House for Mrs. Watson, a lady whose husband was a tea planter in India and who had come home with her children to ensure they benefited from a good Scottish education. There were not many houses in Crieff with an elephant's foot at the door. It held umbrellas and walking sticks though I suspect its original owner would have found a better use for it!

I got on well with Mrs. Watson. She confided in me that *her* elastic had also let her down but she had managed to clutch her breeks through her coat pocket and hirple home. We were sisters in mortification if nothing else.

My duties as usual included cleaning and housework but it was made more pleasurable by the presence of over twenty uniforms billeted there. The lads slept on palliasses on the floor. I don't know where they disappeared to each day but were obviously involved in military manoeuvres and training.

Jean and Bella were both in Perth by this time—Jean in domestic service and Bella producing her second daughter, Kathleen. One Sunday, Jean and I must have been off at the same time for we met up on the South Inch and fancied a shot on the row-boats dancing alluringly on the water. We hesitated. Neither of us had ever rowed before and weren't quite sure what to do. As luck would have it, two soldiers had noticed our indecision and offered to take us out. One was quite a sullen fellow but we took to the other straight away.

"You must come round to my sister's for a cup of tea," said Jean, knowing Bella's door was always open.

Her man, Sandy, a shepherd normally, was now working at Perth Mart and always welcomed the opportunity for a good yarn. Freddie Hill was made more than welcome and we all passed a pleasant afternoon getting acquainted.

Freddie hailed from Sheffield and was one of three brothers. Bill was in the air force, Bernard in the navy and Freddie in the army.

"Now you'll be sure to come back to visit and stay for your dinner", said Bella.

And he promised that he would.

It was over a week later when I was visiting, that I heard the marching of boots and lifted Ishbel, now a toddler, to watch the parade go past. I threw the window up at the very moment fate decreed that Freddie would be passing the house.

"That's me, boys, I'll see you later!"

He hadn't remembered where the house was, as all the streets looked the same to him. He sat down to his first plate of Bella's Scotch Broth.

"I don't know what you call this", he ventured in his thick Yorkshire accent," but it's great!"

Freddie became a great family friend and after the war his parents were to visit Ma in Dallas. They loved the change of air and the friendliness of the folk and Mr. Hill, in particular, loved the freedom to get about the place and explore. On the day he climbed The Wangie, the hill at the end of the village, he returned with a trophy—a tin chantie he had found lying on the path. Great was the speculation as to how it came to be there!

Mr. And Mrs. Hill were a kindly, gentle couple who didn't deserve what life had in store for them. Freddie was sent to North Africa with his unit and while driving his tank along a desert road, went over a land mine. He was blown to pieces. Bill was shot down over France and his body, too, was never found. Of their three sons, carefully spread throughout the forces, only Bernard survived the war. I was in Birmingham visiting the Hills when the telegram arrived to tell these dear people that Freddie had been killed. Poor Mr. Hill. He just about gave up on life after that and never got over their heartbreaking loss.

Why is life often so unfair to those who least deserve it?

It was while I was in Crieff that I received my call-up. I was to go to Glasgow to be trained to handle heavy machinery for the war effort. I stepped off the train at Queen Street and into a swarming throng of people. I'd never seen so many folk in one place before and, for a few seconds, I was quite overwhelmed. It was autumn and the nights were drawing in. It was dull and dreich and, of course, there were no street or shop lights because of the blackout. My training was to take place just off George Square and from there it was easy to take a tram to my digs at the Girl Guide Hostel at Hillhead. I mind the first night I took the tram home, a chap offered to show me my stop and the hostel. Being very much the country mouse, I agreed. When we eventually found my digs, I suspected he wanted something for his trouble. He got a quick peck on the cheek—and nothing more!

With the war on, there was a general perception of being safe amongst your own and I can honestly say I never felt scared. Perhaps I was too trusting but you have to trust people. Most folk are honourable and decent—at least I like to think they are.

I spent about a month in Glasgow and then found myself on a train heading south over the Border. My bike was again in the guard's van.

When I arrived in Birmingham, I first had to find my way out to Selly Oak. I admit to getting lost a few times, but with a good Scots tongue in my head and most Brummies eager to help, I soon found Nellie Johnston's house where I was to share lodgings with an Irish quine called Mary Harkin. Nellie had only one available room and we were to share that. The room had only one available bed—and we were to share that too! You had to make compromises. There was a war on.

Mary and I became very good friends, not because we shared a bed but because she was a country girl like myself and had a sunny and personable disposition. As it turned out, she worked days and I did nights so we had the bed to ourselves when we needed it.

I was employed at The Austin Motor Company and was set to work making parts for wheel nuts for lorries. Initially, I worked one month on day shift, one month on nights. After two months on days, I requested to stay on nights permanently. It was much quieter then and that suited me fine. Background noise always distorted the little hearing I had and made conversation difficult.

I clocked-in at 8 in the evening and out again at 5.30 in the morning. We had a long break around 1 a.m., the equivalent of a lunch hour I suppose, and were often entertained by people singing. I mind one lad had a particularly fine voice. He would sing 'Trees' and bring the noisy canteen to a hush, so beautiful was it.

I travelled in and out to work by tram and surprised myself at how easily I adjusted, not only to factory work but also to life in the second city of England. It was a far cry from Forres!

The machine I used was heavy and unwieldy. The blank nuts were fed in and then a handle was pulled to tighten the chuck. Another lever operated a blade which pared the nut and then it was polished. The final process was the cutting of the thread. That was the trickiest part of the whole operation. Once the drill had bored the hole, a reamer smoothed and polished it and, finally, the thread was cut, rotating the machine to the left or right, depending on the direction required. There were a few wasted nuts before I got the hang of it!

I was in the factory for two and a half years. In the end, however, using such cumbersome machinery for long, protracted periods resulted in damage to my stomach and internal bleeding and I was dispatched to the sick bay for rest and recuperation. The nurse there must have taken pity on me being so far from home and in such a sickly state for she arranged to take me ice-skating when I felt better. Well, what a performance.

I was not a natural!

At first I clung to the side rails scared to move. My bladed feet then took off on their own, each in a different direction, leaving me back-pedalling furiously trying to retrieve them. Gingerly, I made to venture further only to land on my back, arms and legs splayed like a spider with the DT's. Then two lads thought they would give a helping hand. Each took an arm and towed me round the rink. The boots I was wearing were borrowed and too big. Even if they had fitted they wouldn't have been enough to prevent my feet swivelling from side to side in an effort to retain some semblance of stability. Nor would they have conferred on me any hint of decorum or balance. I was screaming my head off as they continued hauling me round and round and, eventually, we all ended in a heap, helpless with laughter and wet with—well anybody's guess! I'd never had such fun before and the hilarity and enjoyment of that night made me feel immeasurably better.

Apart from the skating rink, there were not many opportunities for meeting boys. Most of the lads of my own age were away in France or other theatres of war and the ones that were at home were not always my type. When the chap sitting behind me in the factory offered me a lift home one night, I accepted without realising he might have had motives other than purely altruistic ones. I knew he was married and assumed I would be safe enough in his car. I was wrong! He got more than he bargained for when his hands started exploring but he had the good grace to apologise the following day for his improper behaviour. I was a lot more cautious after that about accepting a lift.

Nellie, my landlady, was the salt of the earth and I became very fond of her. She already had a daughter, Sylvia, and with her man away, had a long wait for her second child. He arrived while I was staying with her and I took great delight in helping her out with shopping and the like. My trusty bike was very useful in nipping down to the shops for supplies and I practised my baby changing and burping skills on the wee lad as often as I was allowed.

Ma would regularly send me fresh chickens and eggs—all the way from Dallas. They were put on the overnight train from Forres and would arrive first thing the next morning. And, do you know, I don't mind on even one egg being broken!

Being on night shift, I would be dead to the world when the postman arrived but, if there was one of Ma's parcels delivered, Nellie would wake me up to open it. She relished the taste of fresh produce in these austere days of rationing and shortages and Ma's generosity and thoughtfulness were toasted often.

With the successful landings on the beaches of Normandy, the war in Europe took a new turn. The Auxiliary Territorial Service (ATS) were to be sent to Belgium now that fighting there had stopped. The Naafi was to follow. The thought of travelling abroad appealed to me so I volunteered my services.

When I was 16, I had told Bella that I wanted to emigrate to Australia and it took her a long time to persuade me that it wasn't a good idea.

"It would be too hard for you, Molly, being deaf and it's too far away," she would say.

Despite that, I knew I wanted to see a bit more of the world than my own wee corner, bonny though it was. This was my chance.

I was sent to Bowlee in Manchester to be trained. I learned later that the head cook had been paid to teach me the principles of cookery but had preferred to pocket the money and leave me to clean out the fires and scrub the pots. A familiar story! Once it dawned on me that this would be my lot if I stayed there, I went to the supervisor and requested to be posted to Belgium. It was by that time deemed safe so I was instructed to get myself to Wales to have a medical and get inoculated. I got my jabs all right but, for some reason, escaped the medical. The next day I arrived at Harwich in my NAAFI uniform and standard issue shoes. I caught the ferry for Belgium that night.

I was met at the pier in Ostend and taken to a very grand hotel on the esplanade. It had been requisitioned as a staff billet and I was there to supervise the cooking! I didn't let on that I hadn't actually had any training and got on with it. It made a change to let others do the most humdrum tasks but I was always mindful of how tedious that could be and mucked in when I could. Local girls were employed as domestic servants and I became very fond of them, especially Lizette and her mum, who would invite me to their home during my time off.

By this time, the hostilities had ended in Europe although fighting continued in the Far East. Ostend was a bustling port with ferries arriving and departing constantly. For some reason, the kitchen in the hotel was on the top floor and we used a lift to take the food downstairs and the dirty dishes back up. One day, shortly after the war had finished, the lift doors opened and, who should be standing there, looking very smart in his uniform, but my cousin, Bill Murray! He was with the supply boats that regularly crossed The Channel and knew I was in Belgium. A few local enquiries later and he had managed to track me down. What an amazing stroke of luck that two Dallas bairns should be in Ostend at the same time! He only had a short time to spend with me but my supervisor kindly let me have the day off and we spent it together.

Most of the local people had a fair idea who had collaborated with the Germans and hated these traitors even more than they did the Nazis. They wanted revenge. The authorities allowed them to do as much damage to homes and possessions as they could in one day. They broke windows, smashed down doors and threw everything they could lift on to the streets. Then they set fire to the lot. The police had forbidden looting of property and, in all honesty, we never saw any sign of it. Bill and I spent the day following them round, fascinated and not a little scared at the intensity of their hatred.

The railway station was down at the docks and gangs of local men gathered there to wait for collaborators to appear. When they did, they seized them and threw them into the water. Each time they surfaced they would push them under until the bubbles had stopped. I had mixed feelings about human beings being murdered like that but could also understand the revulsion behind it. I tried not to dwell on it and forced myself to accept it as an inevitable consequence of war.

Life was never quiet or dull in Ostend at that time. There was a great deal of cleaning up to be done and every effort was being made to eradicate all signs of occupation. The U-boats left behind in the docks had already been scuttled. The bullet holes that peppered the walls and ceilings of our kitchen were to remain for many months, however, and were a constant reminder of the black days of war.

One morning, some of the girls came running into the kitchen.

"Miss Molly, Miss Molly, you must come down to the cellar to take shelter! They're going to blow up the U-boat pens. Come quickly!"

I was in the middle of doing something so, despite their appeals, stayed where I was.

There were two stoves in the kitchen, each supporting a large iron kettle, always on the boil. As the explosives detonated, I watched the kettles slide from one end of the range to the other—and back again. The whole building shook and swayed with the force of the explosion. The sound reverberated for a few seconds and then came the crashing of debris and rushing of water. Then there was silence.

Whether it was as a result of my exposure to these explosions or my hearing just becoming worse over time, I was finding it increasingly more difficult to make out what others were saying and thought a change to the relative quiet of the country would improve things. I requested a move inland but first had to get approval from the M.O.H.

I was shown into a dark room where the doctor sat at one end of a desk and there was another chair for me. On his forehead was a head-torch from which shone a bright light. He started to speak. I could hear his voice but could not make out what he was saying.

"I'm sorry, sir, I can't hear you."

Again, his voice sounded and I could tell he was becoming angry and impatient.

Again, I replied "I'm sorry, sir, I can't hear you."

He got up from his seat and switched on the overhead light. By this time, I had realised that he thought I was trying to feign deafness in an effort to get sent home. He roughly pulled my hair to the side and examined my ears. You've never seen a man change so quickly.

He could not have been nicer.

"Oh, I'm so sorry, my dear. You should never have been passed to come over here with ears like yours. You'll have to go home. Go and see the supervisor and she'll arrange for you to get the next boat back."

I didn't want to go home. I was happy where I was and enjoying the experience of living in another country. I had made many good friends and was having fun. I knew, however, that I had no option and duly went to my supervisor, who sent me to the senior transport officer.

"I know you don't want to go," he said. "There's a boat leaving tomorrow but I'm sure you couldn't possibly be ready in time to catch it. Why don't we put you down for one in ten days' time? Go and see the drivers and tell them to take you with them and try to see as much of the country as you can. It's safe enough now."

And that is what I did.

Over the next week or so, I managed to explore a fair amount of Belgium, getting to Bruges and Ghent and crammed as much as I could into what little time I had. Sadly, the day finally came when I had to leave. I was given a big, beautiful bouquet of flowers and a brass bell with 'Oostende' stamped on it. As the boat pulled out of the docks, I could hear 'Miss Molly, Miss Molly' drifting across the water. Looking over the side-rails I could see all the girls I had worked with lining the sandy spit in front of the hotel. Some were even in the water. Many had pillowcases, others had towels and they were waving and cheering. Through a blur of tears, I waved goodbye to some of the kindest friends I had ever known. When I could no longer see them, I turned and went inside.

I cried my eyes out the whole way home.

## Chapter 21

## I'll Walk Beside You.

When I arrived back in England, I was to report to NAAFI Headquarters on the south coast. I got there late on Friday night.

"Well, Miss Skene, you can go home for the weekend but you must report to your next placement in Ross-shire first thing on Monday morning."

As politely as I could, I pointed out that it would take me all day to get to Dallas and that I would have to spend all day Sunday travelling to Ross-shire. And then I did something quite out of character. I rebelled!

Despite wanting desperately to see Ma and the others, I still felt aggrieved that I had not been allowed to stay in Belgium and I wasn't going to be pushed around any more. I said I wouldn't go to Ross-shire and as the war was over, I could now please myself. Such audacity!

I worked a week's notice, handed back my uniform and found myself a job in a factory in London. Annie was still there so I had somewhere to stay. After a month or so, however, the novelty of being in the big smoke began to fade. Things were different now that the war was over and I no longer found city life as appealing as I had before. Much as I enjoyed Annie's company, I missed the country and so, at the end of the summer of 1945, I returned to Dallas.

The local gamekeeper's wife must have been among those who heard of my return almost as soon as I stepped off the bus for I had barely taken off my coat when there was a knock at the door. She had just had a baby and could I come and help her with the domestic chores? When I realised that would include washing all the towelling nappies by hand and in cold water, I declined.

'International' travel had made me independent and I felt I could get something better than the first offer that came my way. I took the second, though, as I couldn't live with Ma and not pay for my keep. I found a position with Mrs. Gordon at the Longview Hotel in Forres and tried to settle back into some kind of routine. It wasn't easy and as 1946 slipped into '47 without fuss or fanfare, I was beginning to get restless to be off again.

The Labour Exchange found me a position at Stonefield Hotel just outside Inverness and virtually across the road from Bella's sixth or was it tenth home? By this time, her son Robert was already a toddler and the two girls were at school. She was due to produce her fourth at the beginning of the New Year and I was fortunate to be with her when Hazel arrived.

By February, I visited the Labour Exchange again to see if they had anything to suit me.

"There's a position for a housemaid in the north of Shetland," they informed me, "and one at the Station Hotel in Oban."

"Where's that?" I said.

I was soon to find out.

May 1945 was a cauldron of confusion and uncertainty. Everyone from the camps wanted, more than anything, just to get home. Johnny waited patiently at the various holding camps, first in Germany and then in Belgium. He had been transported through Ulm and Munich until eventually he reached Brussels to wait for a plane.

Ever since he left Oban he had written at the top of each page of his army Bible the names of all the places he had passed through. One of these places was Buchenwald but he could never bring himself to dwell on what he had seen there. Finally in Brussels, his turn came to board the Lancaster that was to take him home. He didn't care that his kit bag was jammed in the doors of the bomb bay and that half of his belongings were lost in the Channel. Or that he felt terrified as he flew for the first time in an aircraft that shook and roared with equal ferocity. His only thoughts were of Oban and his much-loved sister and her family. Young Annie, a school girl when he last saw her, was now married with a child of her own and Billy had grown into a fine young man and looked so much like his father.

Once all the paperwork had been written up and the

disembarkation formalities completed, Johnny set off on the long road north. By the time he reached Glasgow it was late in the day. It was the 18th of May and the days in the Highlands were light till nearly midnight. Morning broke around three o'clock, at about the time the mail train for Oban left Queen Street. As it climbed out of the half-light, the mist would have been clearing Ben Lomond and on reaching Crianlarich, the first blush of the new day would be silhouetting Ben More and Stob Binnein. Johnny stood at the carriage door, his neck craning to see it all. By the time he reached Dalmally, he was back in Argyll. He hadn't slept but couldn't bear to take his eyes from the scene. Loch Awe, Taynuilt, Connel Ferry passed in a moment and soon the train was at the Summit. As it coasted past Glencruitten and down Soroba Hill, the outline of the bay came into view. Behind, the mountains of Mull, ancient and enduring, rose up to form a familiar outline. And then, after years of longing, there she was, still asleep save for a few twinkling lights but nestling, as he had left her, between the hills and the sea.

Oban.

As the train pulled into the station, the fishing boats bobbed and nodded their welcome beside the pier and the seagulls chorused their hellos. The smell of the sea filled his head and the rush of the familiar became almost too much to bear.

And there on the platform stood Alastair, his cherished brother-in-law. The two held each other for a long while. There was no need for words.

— The train pulled into the station at ten o'clock. It was February and I had been the only passenger on board. My bike was, yet again, in the guard's van and the guard was in the carriage keeping me company. The Station Hotel, as you might expect, was across the road from the railway station and it didn't take me long to find my way. The first person I met was the head porter who made to take my case, assuming I was a guest.

"Could I see the housekeeper?" I asked and he dropped the case at my feet.

I was taken upstairs to a room I was to share with Sheila Green, an Irish girl. Next door was Mary MacDonald, a Highlander, and both girls were to become very dear friends.

There was no time to ease gently into my new position as Curstan Black's wedding reception was being held the following day. Her sisters, Isobel and Nancy had decorated the tables and the splash of colour and sight of fresh spring flowers brightened the room and offered a respite from the uniform grey of post-war life. I was allocated the job of waiting at the tables and lending a hand to whatever task needed attending to and, even on that first day in Oban, I could tell that the people were friendly and kind—most of them, anyway.

My main role was to be housemaid and I was responsible for three floors of rooms, all in one wing of the hotel. Guests would occasionally stay for a fortnight or more but often would only need accommodation for one night between arriving from Glasgow on the late train and leaving for Mull on the early ferry. One such regular traveller was Lady M. who was a person of elegance and charm and who always showed her appreciation by leaving a half crown tip. At least, she seemed to tip everyone but me. Eventually I became suspicious, although that was not normally in my nature. One morning after she had left I went into the room and, sure enough, there was my tip lying on the dressing-table. I put it in my pocket, pulled the door over slightly and went into the unlit linen cupboard next door. I did not have long to wait. The head porter's silhouette moved around the room and, after hesitating a while, made to leave. The shock he got as he came out of the gloom was only equalled by the anger I felt at being cheated.

"Did she leave you anything?" he stammered.

"Yes, she did, and it's in my pocket!"

My wages were not very great, certainly not as much as he earned, but he had felt no compunction at stealing from me. It cast a shadow over my time there.

One of the other porters fancied himself and his chances. On the day he came up to my floor and made to trap me in the mattress store, he had more than stock-taking on his mind! Whether he tried out his unwelcome advances on all the other girls or thought that a deaf country quine would be a push-over, I never found out but, as I shut the store cupboard door behind me, he was the one lying sprawled and dishevelled on the floor with his gas at a peep and his ardour defused. He never forgave me for rejecting him and soon found a way to get his revenge.

If any of the staff wanted to be out later than ten when the front door was locked, they had to request a late pass and obtain a key from the desk. The porter would usually be hanging about and, on the night that I first went to the badminton club, he overheard me asking for the key. I went out and had an enjoyable evening only spoiled when I arrived back at the hotel. Despite the key turning in the lock, the door refused to budge. I tried several times before resigning myself to a cold night sitting on the stone step. And then two bobbies came round the corner. I explained my predicament and they tried the key. They met with the same result and couldn't fathom why the door wouldn't open. Not to be defeated, I asked them to accompany me round to the back of the hotel which was actually on George Street, the main thoroughfare of the town. All the deliveries were brought there to save using the guest entrance—provisions, laundry, beer and——— coal!

"Now," I said to the policemen, "if you would just lift this," pointing to the metal grating lying straddling the pavement, "I'll let myself down and get in that way."

And they did just that. I clambered over the coal heap and went to bed.

In the morning, the girls were all keen to know how I'd got on and whom I'd met.

"What time did you get in?" they enquired.

"Oh, long after you were sound asleep," said I.

The porter said nothing but kept looking at me.

The following week, I again asked for a key and was overheard. Again, the key refused to open the door but this time the coal grating had been padlocked. Word had obviously got out that the hotel could be accessed this way. I refused to be beaten and started to use my climbing skills that had been honed to an art on the roof of Branchill. Up the drain pipe I sprachled and dived head first through the small window on the first floor. It was then easy enough to make my way to my room. But first, I nipped downstairs to check the door. The key wasn't faulty. The door had been locked as I expected but someone had pushed the snib across, making entry impossible. I was in no doubt as to who the culprit was.

The same interrogation from my workmates followed the next morning and the same light-hearted replies from me. The porter hovered about, baffled and perplexed, looking at me either in admiration or, I suspect, unease. His brain was obviously trying to work out just how I had got in. I never gave him the satisfaction of telling him.

Apart from the slight difficulties at work, I liked living in Oban.

The townsfolk made me feel very welcome and would invite me to Bohemian Teas, Guilds and the like. I particularly enjoyed the badminton club. A young man had taken my fancy. I made sure that I was his partner as often as the chance arose and before long, he asked me to go for a walk with him.

It wasn't easy adjusting back to civilian life. Johnny, like the other returning Prisoners of War, was given permission to be absent from his unit for all of seven weeks, after almost five years of imprisonment. He then had to report back to headquarters in Perth and go through the process of being demobbed. It was not until 7$^{th}$ August that he was finally released from military service. Not quite finally. He was placed on the Royal Army Reserve List and remained there for a further nine years. He was given a demob suit—a token of appreciation from a grateful nation—and a civic reception from the Provost and councillors of Oban. And that was it.

The malnutrition and ill health he had suffered took many years to heal. Some of the mental scars never left but he was resilient and got on with it. Jobs were in short supply and he applied for many before being accepted by the Post Office as a trainee for the first two years until he earned the right to wear a uniform. He gradually picked up the threads of his old life but much of the familiar was gone. He couldn't expect it to be any other way and raw grief surfaced regularly when he remembered his comrades that hadn't made it home.

The Pipe Band was still there and he could lose himself in the music and forget the past for a while. During the winter nights, the badminton league had resumed and that was good for keeping fit and meeting girls. There was one new lassie had appeared towards the end of the spring of 1948 and Johnny had taken quite a shine to her. He made sure he partnered her as often as the chance arose and found he liked her a lot. After a few weeks, he plucked up the courage to ask her to go for a walk with him.

# Post Script

Molly and Johnny were married in Castlehill Church, Forres in the summer of 1949.

Fate, luck and circumstance had brought them together. Only death would now part them.

Just before they were married, Johnny requested a song dedicated to her to be played on the wireless and John McCormack's beautiful, tenor voice sang,

"I'll walk beside you through the passing years,

Through days of cloud and sunshine, joy and tears.

And when the great call comes, though sunset gleams

I'll walk beside you to the land of dreams."

And he did.

# Sources and Further Reading.

The Moray Book   Donald Omand   Paul Harris Publishing

Record of the Parish of Dallas   Robert Douglas   Moray Heritage Centre

Farm Life in North-East Scotland  1840-1914  Ian Carter
John Donald Publishers

3rd Statistical Account of Scotland -Counties of Moray and Nairn
Henry Hamilton   Collins Publishers

The Dallas Raid   Rev. J.G. Murray   Rafford Local Collection, Elgin Library.

Forres and Area, Past and Present   Mike Seton   Local Collection

Fermfolk and Fisherfolk   John Smith and David Stevenson
Aberdeen University Press

Forres, Elgin and Nairn Gazette

Elgin Courant and Courier

The Northern Scot

The Parish of Dallas   James Mitchell

A compilation of the history of Dallas   Ian Sutherland

Agricultural Hand Tools   Roy Brigden   Shire Publications

Scottish Agricultural Implements   Bob Powell   Shire Publications

Rafford in the Past   T.L. Mason   Local Collection, Elgin Library

Moray-----Province and People   W.D.H. Sellar   Local Collection, Elgin Library

Wells and Waterfalls   Robert Douglas   Local Collection, Elgin Library

Morayshire Described   J. and W. Watson   Local Collection, Elgin Library

Moray and Nairn   County Histories of Scotland   Charles Rampini
William Blackwood and Sons.

The Birds of Moray and Nairn    Martin Cook    Mercat Press, Edinburgh.

The Flora of Moray, Nairn and East Inverness    Mary McCallum Webster
Aberdeen University Press.

The History of the Argyll and Sutherland    Highlanders $8^{th}$ Battalion.
Lt.-Col. A.D. Malcolm    Nelson

Argyllshire Highlanders    1860-1960    Lt.-Col. G.I. Malcolm
The Halberd Press

The Highland Division    Mr.Eric Linklater.    H.M.S.O.

St.Valery-The Impossible Odds    Mr. Bill Innes.    Birlinn

No Cheese after Dinner    Mr. Fred Kennington.

Churchill's Sacrifice of the Highland Division    Mr. Saul David.    Brassey's

Lightning Source UK Ltd.
Milton Keynes UK
UKOW031043011111

181283UK00002B/33/P